Ahmed walked slowly toward her

Her voice shook as Leonie asked, ''Why have you had me come all this way in this unexpected fashion? Without the courtesy of coming properly to ask me.''

''I have brought you here because I wanted to do so. Does that answer your question?''

Aghast at that tone, those words, Leonie found she couldn't answer for a moment, then she said, ''I don't understand why you're acting like this!'' All the anger she'd been feeling on that long ride disintegrated. Somehow she was frightened. But this was the Ahmed whom she had loved.

''Surely you don't mind?'' said that grating silken voice. ''You have shown me on other occasions that you are not averse to my presence . . . or even to my lovemaking.''

Mons Daveson remembers sending off her first manuscript after a great deal of work—only to have it rejected. She is now, however, a seasoned author who appreciates the pleasures and frustrations that come with writing. "There is a certain feeling you get when you start a story," she explains, "a story that has been building, little by little, segment by segment, within the mind, and see the actual words written down." It is a feeling of satisfaction once all the sentences and paragraphs finally come together. Mons grew up in the ruggedly beautiful Australian outback, has visited all parts of her country and now lives with her family in Brisbane.

DESERT INTERLUDE
Mons Daveson

Harlequin Books

TORONTO • NEW YORK • LONDON
AMSTERDAM • PARIS • SYDNEY • HAMBURG
STOCKHOLM • ATHENS • TOKYO • MILAN

Original hardcover edition published in 1990
by Mills & Boon Limited

ISBN 0-373-17091-2

Harlequin Romance first edition August 1991

DESERT INTERLUDE

CHAPTER ONE

SHE stood there, young, fair, feeling abandoned—
even if looking completely self-possessed amid the
crowded, bustling swirl of movement all about her. It
was an alien environment that was surrounding her
too.

She gazed at the busy, hurrying tourists, some
waiting, as she was, to be met, or for their luggage to
come out on the carousel. But most of all she looked
at the airport workers so foreignly clad in ankle-length
coffee-coloured robes. At other men too, even if
discreetly, with the long floating material draping them
also—with the difference that these gowns were in
pristine white.

It was only carefully that she gazed at these last,
haughty, frightening-looking fierce men, with their
white kaffiyehs hiding almost all their countenance,
allowing only the front face and profile to be seen.
These people appeared to show no interest whatsoever
in the frenetic crush swirling about them. She wondered when the person who was to meet her would
show up.

'Miss Saunders?' The two words caused her to swing
round to gaze at the young man addressing her. She
breathed with relief. This was someone she could
relate to—ordinary, nice, and showing a casual groom-
ing that said it all. She said, 'Yes, I'm Leonie
Saunders.' She smiled at him.

'And I'm Greg Coughlan, from the Embassy. I'm to
take you to the hospital to meet Mrs Hailstrom.'

The smile on the girl's face reached upwards to make dark blue eyes grow brighter. She said, 'The Embassy, no less! I *am* honoured!'

The grin she received back was of the same quality. 'No, I don't think it is you who are being honoured. We just do all we can for Mrs Hailstrom. She is a very popular lady around our place. Look, the luggage is beginning to arrive. Point yours out.'

'I only have one large case. . .and this small one.' She gestured towards the zipped overnight case at her feet. She broke off to say, 'There it is!' but it had gone past.

And then suddenly there was unexpectedly both commotion and quietness in the area surrounding them. Soldiers were making a path through the crowd. Not violently or with any force, but clearing a path just the same.

Greg Coughlan glanced quickly across to where Leonie was watching, then stretched out a hand to draw her more firmly back. She continued to look, wondering.

A small group of men were walking from a far door, probably a VIP lounge. Four of them white-clad in burnous and kaffiyeh, walked on either side of two Arabs and a khaki-clad officer who had a major's pips on his shoulders.

She saw also that the elder one of the two Arabs had a gold cord, like—if a little more ornate than— the ones the four bodyguards were wearing around their white headdress. It was obvious that he was the important personage in the way he carried himself, in the dark haughty countenance with its close-cut black beard and fierce-looking eyes.

Leonie saw her companion smile and nod to the soldier, who raised his hand in a salute; and then, as that hawklike face followed his aide's glance and looked at them also, Greg stood straighter, and half bowed.

Then to her, just a silent onlooker, only interested in them as were half a hundred people around them, she saw the second Arab's head turn and he was gazing directly at them. As his companion was, he also was clad in pristine white, but around his kaffiyeh was bound a twisted cord of black and silver. From its concealment emerged a chiselled profile that seemed to match the marble heads she had seen only yesterday in the museums in Athens.

Under black arched brows, dark eyes whose colour she could not distinguish glanced at them both but appeared to see neither. And sculptured lips which could also have been chiselled from marble neither smiled nor gave greeting, the whole countenance giving the impression of remote unawareness.

Then, unexpectedly, a dark tanned hand was lifted to the man standing behind her, and Greg was bowing again, if not so deeply. But the gaze from that incredibly handsome, expressionless face had moved, passing over her as if over empty space—and not wanting it, not expecting it, Leonie felt suddenly the pulsing jolt deep inside that sent her every nerve fluttering.

Then the small group had passed, and the airport was again going about its own business. Leonie remained motionless, aware that Greg was asking her a question, but was unable to hear or take in its meaning.

What had happened just now? She really wasn't an impressionable schoolgirl just out of the schoolroom. She had been working as a doctor's receptionist for the three years since leaving school at eighteen, and had lived the usual social life of any attractive young female. Maybe she had not lived as fully as had done many of her contemporaries, but that was something she had hoped might happen in the future when a man she liked—or loved—did come along. There was no hurry.

She found she had to take a deep steadying breath. She knew that never before had such a condition overcome her. Shaking her head to clear from its vision a glance from impersonal eyes which had seemed not even to have noticed her, she muttered, 'Oh, I'm mad!'

An impatient exclamation from her companion brought her attention abruptly back to where she was. Answering his terse question, she told him, 'Yes, that's the one,' and, as he reached out and caught hold of the large case, she bent to pick up the small one at her feet. Then, with her big shoulder-bag carelessly slung, she walked through this strange airport of Cairo to begin a new life for the next two months.

The road into the city went arrow-straight into the distance, but from its car window Leonie saw that this was indeed the East. Passers-by walking beside it in their long robes and their black, altogether enveloping garments gave the explicit impression of an alien scene. She watched it, enchanted.

Suddenly, however, she found she had to bring her attention to the man beside her. He was saying, 'We turn off now to the hospital, Leonie, to collect Mrs Hailstrom and take you to your hotel. Of course, being who she is, she'll be staying at Shepheards, not the Hilton or some such hotel.'

'What exactly do those words, or, more important, does that tone mean, Greg? It sounded strange the way you spoke.'

'No, it wasn't at all.' Greg was giving his attention

to the road opening up before him as he turned off the main highway. It was crowded with traffic—actually it was overcrowded. He added then, 'Oh, only that Shepheards is a landmark of old Cairo. Built and used by us when we were here in Egypt, it was a famous place—like Raffles is in Singapore, or the Grand in Colombo. But Egyptians run it now.'

There didn't seem much she could answer to that, so she changed the subject, asking tentatively, off-handedly, 'Who were those people you greeted at the airport, Greg? They appeared to be very important. Do they belong to the Government?'

Her companion hesitated a minute before replying, then said, 'No, they're not Government members, not of Egypt—although they most likely work closely with it. The older one is Prince Saud from Saudi Arabia, and the soldier is his aide-de-camp. I've met them at our Embassy at social functions. . .' Greg's words trailed off as he scanned the kerb seeking a parking slot. He did not mention the second Arab.

Unable to prevent herself, Leonie asked, 'Is the other one a Saudi Arabian too? By his looks and manner, he too could well be a prince.'

'No, he's the Sheikh Ahmed Wallifa, an Arab from the interior.' Without continuing, Greg parked, and coming round to open her door, looked directly down at her as they both stood on the pavement. He said, 'Look, Leonie,' and he spoke seriously, 'I know you don't come under our Embassy's jurisdiction, being an Australian, but this is the advice I'd give if you did. . .

'I like Egypt, I'm enjoying very much my stint in this country. However, like many young girls, you mustn't come to it starry-eyed, expecting what used to be called the Romantic East. It's a country only now this last half-century endeavouring to bring itself—and its customs—into the modern world. But believe me, those older customs still apply among the majority of them. So don't be misled by handsome Arab princes, which that man you enquired about is in his own world. His mother might have been a Greek lady, but he himself is an Arab of the Arabs, believe me. And— he's not the sort of person you should ever be thinking about.'

'Why are you saying this to me, Greg? Why should I care about what he is? I don't even remember one particular person, except that there were two Arabs in the centre of that group who had a way made for them as they passed through the airport back there.' Leonie told the lie unblushingly, and made her manner non-chalant as they both turned to enter the hospital.

But she did see that Greg had turned a sceptical face towards her, although he said nothing else. Then after traversing a corridor and ascending some stairs they entered a room where a nurse was packing a case.

'Here's Leonie Saunders, Mrs Hailstrom,' said Greg.

The elderly woman with her arm in a sling gazed at Leonie. 'Hello, my dear. It's good of you to come along to help me,' she said.

'Oh no, I'm the lucky one,' answered Leonie. 'I was thrilled at the idea of being able to come to Egypt. But you have been told, haven't you, that I'm not a trained nurse? That I was only available because I'd escorted a patient to England, and was then on my way home.'

'My dear girl, I have your background from A to Z, from that old goat in London I've known for fifty years. I think we'll deal very well together. You have only to see that my maid Sunna does the things which are necessary.'

The forthright old lady turned then to the nurse,

and it was just as well she had done so, for Leonie was standing there with her mouth actually fallen open. To so describe the very distinguished orthopaedic surgeon who had recruited her for this job was scandalous. . .an old goat, indeed! She forced her lips together and turned to face the argument now going on.

Knowing that with this woman, if she were to accomplish what she had been sent here for, she had better begin at the beginning, Leonie said, 'The nurse is right, Mrs Hailstrom. You bump that arm or even fall a little and you're going to be sorry. So I'm afraid it must be the wheelchair. We'll all go down in the lift instead of the stairs. You'll find that even a trip to the hotel will tire you now.'

She motioned to the nurse, and saw with relief that her new employer was subsiding into the conveyance brought to her. An amused voice said softly into her ear, 'I would never have believed it!'

But as they followed the wheelchair and its attendant out and along the corridor, Greg continued, 'We at the Embassy are often invited up to the Hailstrom estate at Aswan. It's a much sought-after invitation, However, I'll tell you this, I can't think of anyone else with the nerve to tell her what to do.'

'Oh, but she's been in hospital, and in pain. Sensibly she realises that what professionals tell her is for her own good. In my job at home, I meet many such patients returning for checks and X-ray results, so what I told Mrs Hailstrom is true and she probably knows it.'

Leonie met a sister and was given medication for the next three weeks. Repeating the instructions, she received a satisfied nod from the starched and severe-looking woman, and then they were on their way to whatever Egypt had in store for her.

Her eyes shining, her face enchanted, she gazed out at the alien scene sliding past. From the back seat her new employer must have been watching her. She said, 'You seem to like it here. That's one thing for me to be thankful for. I couldn't have borne having someone around me who disliked the place while waiting for me to recover. And that reminds me, Greg, my boy. We'll be here for another week, so you can take Leonie out to a night-club or restaurant one night. But mind you, in a party. I don't trust you on your own!'

'Me and my reputation!' sighed Greg. 'I only wish it were true. But OK, I'll do that. Still, I'll have to watch where I take her. It won't do to encourage the idealistic attitude she has to this country. Also, I demand my *quid pro quo*. If I take Leonie out for you, I claim the right to the first invitation you send out from Aswan when you're better.'

'Done!' came from the back seat, and Leonie turned round, wondering. Why would an attractive and, on his own admission, a dedicated career man like this one driving them angle for such an invitation? From what she had seen of him she imagined he would be snowed under with all kinds of them. And Mrs Hailstrom *was* an old lady.

That same old lady looked back at her and grinned, understanding completely the expression on the girl's face. She told her, 'They enjoy coming up to my place, away from intrigues and work, and other Embassy people. There are horses to ride, feluccas to sail the river, tennis, and sometimes excursions into the desert. Also, I think they like my home—and my food.'

'Don't we just! Right, it's a deal. But look, here we are.'

Leonie looked. It didn't seem much to be a landmark, she thought. But, descending from the car which had been opened by a porter in the ubiquitous long coffee-coloured djibbah, she saw that between buildings was a glimpse of water.

She had time for seeing no more. She said, standing at the back door, 'Turn, and come out feet first, Mrs Hailstrom. I'll watch your arm.'

Then all three were facing the façade of the famous Shepheards Hotel. Greg dropped his keys into the hand of the man waiting for them, and they walked up the low steps.

But suddenly, extraneous thoughts about this place were gone with the wind as Leonie gazed about the large foyer into which she had stepped, gazed enchanted at the marble floor with its great stylised motif catching at everyone's attention—this floor she had seen being danced on in a famous movie.

A man was coming forward to meet them. Dressed in a suit that shouted Saville Row, he took hold of Mrs Hailstrom's hand and bowed slightly over it. He greeted Greg, and then, as her employer added, 'This is Miss Leonie Saunders, Mr Hamid, who has kindly come to help look after me,' he bent that gleaming dark head in the slightest of bows, then turned, speaking to Greg, who was leaving.

Leonie grinned to herself. There had been definitely no hand taken this time. Maybe her lowly status was the reason, or the fact that she was a young female. But what did she care? She was here in Egypt, the land of the Pharaohs.

Greg was saying over a shoulder, 'I'll be in touch. So long!'

A finger was snapped. Hands reached down to gather up luggage which had been brought inside, and in a small group they made their way to the lifts.

Leonie found she had no need to worry about any

arm being jostled. They had one elevator, the suitcases
and their bearers another. She said, 'Take your arm
out of its sling, Mrs Hailstrom. The weight of it
hanging down will help the break.' She was sent a
dubious look, but the arm did come out.

Along a deep-carpeted corridor they went. A door
was opened and they were motioned through. Leonie
noticed that her own luggage went into the next room.
Someone must be able to read labels.

Inside the large suite, her employer said, 'This is
Sunna,' as she indicated a small dark woman who was
coming towards them. 'She's been with me for many
years and, with you, will be looking after me.' Leonie
smiled warmly into the dark wrinkled face, said hello,
then gazed round the large, deeply carpeted room.
She saw that it opened out on to a balcony through big
glass sliding doors, and couldn't prevent herself from
going across to them. There had been a glint of water.

Yes, outside, across from a railed-in veranda she
saw the Nile. The river whose mystique men had
fantasised about down through countless ages. Mrs
Hailstrom came to stand beside her, and they gazed
on it over a road crowded with rushing cars, over a
footpath running beside it, with the branches of trees
throwing on it both light and shade.

Leonie said dreamily, 'Just think of the craft which
have sailed on its waters! Pharaohs in their golden
barges, bandits slave-trading under their swift sails,
and later armies, some of them belonging to us, Mrs
Hailstrom. What tales it could tell!'

She drew a deep, breath, and turning, found herself
being watched, not the Nile. She laughed, embarrassed
a little.

'You know, Leonie, that's how I feel about it

too. . .but it's different to hear those ideas coming from a young girl living so far away.'

'Oh,' Leonie laughed again, 'I expect it's only because I've read so much history. We lived in the outback on a small property until my father was killed, and then, having to let it go, went to Brisbane when I was twelve, where my mother died five years later. My mother. . .' here her words trailed off for a moment, then she finished, 'never recovered from my father's death, and was glad to go, I think. I stayed at home with her as much as I could, and that I suppose is the reason I read books when I should have been out socialising.

'Look,' in an abruptly different tone of voice, Leonie resumed, 'the river has taken on another colour. Look at those white sails against its coming darkness!'

'Yes, the sun is going, it will be night soon,' said Mrs Hailstrom. 'You know, I love this place, this hotel. I came here as a bride of nineteen. We'd just arrived when war was declared. I've been in Egypt ever since, except for a few trips home. And, broken arm or not, advice to the contrary or not, I'm damned well going to stay here!'

Surprised, Leonie swung round at the fierce tone. 'But a broken arm shouldn't force you to leave, surely, if you don't want to? Broken bones get better, if you take care. And we'll see that you do take care.' Leonie's tone too had taken on a little fierceness.

'Yes, we will, won't we, between the two of us. But for now we're going inside to dress for dinner, and then we'll go upstairs to the restaurant. I'm tired of having meals on trays and in bedrooms!'

CHAPTER TWO

THE sound beat in through the open window; the figure lying so still in the small narrow bed stirred, then came awake to open eyes on unfamiliar surroundings as that echo came again.

Aware suddenly of where she was, Leonie wondered if that sound which had awakened her was the call of the muezzin—but it had gone. She got out of bed and pattered on bare feet across to the window—not a great glass sliding door like the one in the next suite, but a large glass window, none the less.

The river was before her, and low, slanting, horizontal beams of early sunlight were painting the water a fiery crimson in places, leaving the stain of dark pewter in others. A large white sail skimmed swiftly past, and she stood watching it, remembering last night.

They had come inside from the balcony and, helped to dress, her employer had slipped into a loose gold and orange caftan. Leaving Sunna to complete the rest of her mistress's toilette, Leonie had gone to her own room to unpack.

Hanging away dresses and skirts, she had left jeans and shorts in her case. 'When in Rome do as the Romans do' was a good axiom. Then, quickly showering, she donned a cool cotton frock in lemon and white. As she finished her own toilette, she wondered, even if involuntarily, if she would ever see a certain man again. After all, as Greg had told her, this was the hotel the Egyptians used.

Don't be stupid, she admonished herself. She would

never see him again; but she knew it would take a long time for that sculptured countenance to fade from her memory—or that cord which had seemed to stretch between them across that crowded room to wither and disintegrate, because it *had* been there.

Then she shook her head, dismissing the memory of the incident. There might have been interest on her side, but the man had simply seen space where she had been standing.

A last check of her appearance, a last look at pink-shaded lips, at fair shining hair turned under just above her shoulders with a fringe shadowing dark blue eyes, and she was turning, making for the next suite.

They had strolled companionably along the deep-carpeted corridor, Mrs Hailstrom saying good evening in Arabic to the porter at his hallway station. And on the top floor, stepping out of the lift, they went out to the roof-garden first to look out over the city and then back to enter the dining-room, long, deep, and colourful, its waiters in their ankle-length coffee-coloured djibbahs, its *maître d'* in crimson jacket and gold cumerbund advancing to meet them, a scene from the East.

'Mrs Hailstrom, I've put you and Miss Saunders by the window where you will be away from any jostling,' the dark, smiling elderly man told them.

He beckoned, and a waiter led them to their table, which was beside a window. After ordering from the large menu offered, Leonie pushed aside a little the fragile orange curtain beside her. The curtains gave, she guessed, an added glow to the vivid golden tone of the restaurant, and beyond, far down, she saw the lights, the uncounted lights, which coloured this city of Cairo by night.

Mrs Hailstrom was managing quite competently with

a fork, so, making a play with her own, Leonie glanced surreptitiously about her. There were men dressed like another man she remembered. There were also men in business suits, tourists with their womenfolk beside them—but not the figure she was seeking. And, deep down, she had not really expected it to be there.

So they ate their dinner, and, back in her employer's room to check that all was well, Leonie swung round on hearing the dismay Mrs Hailstrom's voice carried when next she spoke.

'What is it?' she enquired sharply.

'I must have left my glasses upstairs. I know I didn't need them in the restaurant, so where could they have got to? I. . .oh, yes, I do know where they are. I had the case in my hand when we were out on the roof-garden gazing out over the town. Good heavens, I wonder if they've been picked up or knocked over. I'd better ring through to the restaurant for someone to be sent out to see if they're still there.'

Leonie flipped a hand. 'No, don't,' she said. 'It will be quicker if I go. If they're still there I know exactly where we stood. If they're not, I'll go inside and ask. One thing,' here she grinned across at the older woman, 'the staff will know who I'm talking about when I ask for *your* glasses!' Leonie was speaking over a shoulder as she made for the door.

Once again she trod the long corridor, took the lift, and moving through the restaurant ante-room, kept her glance straight before her. It was crowded with men now, Egyptian men, with not many tourists there. She walked straight through, head high, gazing at no one, and pushed open the glass doors.

A man in long pristine white robes was leaning against the far parapet, his back towards her, gazing out and down. For just the barest second her feet remained rooted to the tiled floor, her will unable to send them forward. Then taking a deep breath, she told herself not to be stupid.

Every Arab dressed in white wasn't the man to whom her thoughts automatically flowed. There were natives in the next room dressed in such garments, as well as in dark business suits. She shrugged, and made herself move forward, towards where the glasses should be, and where that motionless form was leaning.

She got closer, her sandalled feet making no noise. But it seemed the man must have heard something, for his body straightened like an uncoiled spring as he swung round. That austere face, those hooded eyes looked her over. He didn't speak, so Leonie made herself do so. 'I've come for some glasses which were left there on the ledge,' she said, pointing.

They were there beside him but she couldn't make herself reach out and collect them. Then long brown fingers handed them across, and a voice—an English voice, she realised, startled—said, 'You were lucky they're not down there.' He pointed over the parapet.

'Yes, I know,' answered Leonie, and knew also that she should take the small case and go. But she said without volition, 'When I looked over there earlier, I was amazed at the thousands of cars. Cairo seems so modern. I've always thought of it as a city of the East.'

She was looked over once again, and that voice speaking in English said softly, 'You should realise it *is* a city of the East. The modernity as yet is only a covering.' The voice paused for a moment, then resumed, 'And young ladies shouldn't go racing around it by themselves, as you seem to be doing.'

'I am *not* racing around on my own!' began Leonie indignantly, but the man had suddenly gazed beyond

her at what seemed a stir in the other room. He said,
'You'd better go,' and turned away.

Back with Mrs Hailstrom, Leonie had handed over
the glasses, then went to her own room. But those
were all memories of last night. Today was a new day
just coming alive, and she decided she was going to
see as much of this city as she could. So, quickly
dressing in the skirt and blouse which she considered
her working uniform, she was outside, locking her
door, and making for the lifts.

Downstairs, she trod over the vast marble floor
where cleaners were at work. They stood out of her
way and smiled as she went through. For a moment,
standing in the bright sunlight, she remained on the
top step gazing about her. Then, turning deliberately,
she walked down the side of the hotel. She walked
past the group of dragomen, taxi-drivers, and other
tourist appendages who had connections with
Shepheards, and who were congregated there waiting
for the day's trade.

There was quite a group and their dark gaze followed her, but she was from the hotel and as such she
walked straight ahead along the footpath, sweeping
her glance impersonally over them all with a murmured good morning.

She was aware that they would probably still be
watching her, and was thankful when she crossed the
road to the river and they were lost to sight around a
bend.

On the river footpath, she turned to walk upwards,
along what seemed a more deserted area, the down-
ward direction cluttered with buildings and boats. So
strolling, her face up to the breeze wafting from across
the water, she smiled inside herself. How lucky she

was to be here enjoying herself, she thought—and it had come about so accidentally.

Three small boys, also dressed in the ankle-length fashion, rushed past her, their high excited voices echoing back. No one else appeared to be using this beautiful river walkway so early in the morning; but this was a tourist area, and the comings and goings would begin much later.

Yet here was something different, Leonie thought, as she came to and then passed a launch moored to a jetty running from the bank to where its gangplank came down. As she strolled past she looked it over— from its sleek, pristine white sides, to the gleam of polished brass and woods. A rich man's toy, she surmised, but oh, so lovely to look at.

A glance at her watch further along caused her to turn her footsteps homeward, if reluctantly. It was seven o'clock, and although she had been informed that Mrs Hailstrom would be served early morning tea, she intended to be there for when she was dressing.

Still sauntering, her glance on this river about which she had read so much, key dangling from a finger, she suddenly turned. A small donkey braying loudly was galloping at full steam towards her. She didn't like it on this small footpath, and moved over against the railings away from its passage.

A yell, echoing violently from behind, only made it go faster, and, galloping past, it knocked her flying.

She didn't see the three young boys racing along trying to catch up. She had been thrown through the railings, but only on to the top of the bank. Endeavouring to rise, she looked down the steep incline and knew she had lost her key.

Flustered, tumbled about, she got to one knee.

Then, frightened suddenly, she tried to swing away as a strong brown hand gripped her shoulder. She found she couldn't do anything else except what that hand wanted her to do. She felt its strength through her entire system.

But still she attempted to remove herself from that iron-hard grasp. Panicking now about the presence of whoever was behind her, about being alone in this empty alien place, she turned. . .and looked directly into brilliant green eyes set in a handsome face. A face she had seen before.

But this time, only anger showed on that austere countenance, and as she again tried to pull away she found that that strong hard hand was propelling her along the small jetty and on to the launch she had admired earlier this morning.

Again, automatically she tried to push the hand from her shoulder. It was an instinctive reaction, even if it was against a man whose image had been with her as she sought sleep last night. But this *was* a strange boat, this man *was* an Arab. . .

A voice from above said something sharply in Arabic, then the man had turned towards her, saying, 'Try to use what common sense you have, Miss Saunders. If you want to go back to the hotel looking as if you've been partaking in a public brawl, be my guest. If not, come downstairs before you are the cynosure of every passing eye.'

The hand on her shoulder propelled her forward. She went! What else could she do on hearing those words—words that were uttered in such a hard, contemptuous tone.

She knew she passed through an elegant saloon. She knew that now she was standing in a bathroom, but she only stood looking directly at the man holding her.

He had spoken in English, in his unaccented, softly spoken English.

He said now, 'Wash your hands!'

Leonie gazed down at them and saw that they were covered with dirty, sticky mud, with one of her pink-polished nails broken. She turned from that classical, smooth brown face, clean-shaven even at this early hour, from that figure dressed as it had been yesterday in pristine white, and ran water into the bowl.

But she just looked at it, unable to make herself proceed further, shock and distress taking over her natural competence.

He had called her Miss Saunders, so he must know who she was! But how could he? He had seen her once, at the airport, and again last night in the roof-garden. How could he know?

He said again, 'Wash your hands!' Impatience was now colouring the words. She washed and scrubbed them, allowing the running water to rinse them clean. As he began to speak again, she raised her eyes to meet his glance in the mirror.

'Now your face,' that curt but soft voice said. It didn't sound soft when it was speaking in Arabic.

Her gaze met his in the reflecting glass, blue eyes meeting deep green. Yes, there was a large smear of earth on one cheek, put there most likely while she used a hand to lever herself from the ground.

She said to that reflected, immaculate form leaning so indolently against the door frame, 'I can manage now, thank you!'

He didn't go away. He said, 'No doubt you can, but I haven't a lot of time. Wash your face.'

Outraged, Leonie wished she could wipe some of the mud over him. She would dearly love to make a mess of *his* clothes! After all, hers had been just as fresh when she had set out.

Whether he read her expression or not, his own changed, and his figure straightened abruptly against the wood behind him.

Seeing an altogether different look in a suddenly changed countenance, Leonie reached down, and cupping water, washed her face. Eyes closed, she reached blindly for a towel, and found one put into her seeking hands.

Not delicately patting her skin dry, she rubbed at it violently. 'Damn him,' she muttered into the towel, 'why doesn't he go away and let me get on with it— seeing that I have to!'

'Finish the job and clean the mud off your skirt,' she was told. She glanced down, saw the smear spread across the hemline, then reached for a small folded white towel, and scrubbed.

Upright again, and without any prompting this time from that lounging figure, she bypassed two brushes and picked up a long slender comb. Passing it back and forth under a running tap, she dried it on a towel, then combed her hair until it was set in its natural shining shape.

She carefully washed the comb again and put it back in its place. Was it amusement she saw far back in that hard, proud face, whose only outward expression seemed to be impersonal, remote?

'Well now,' that so English voice said, 'you're presentable enough to return to the hotel, where every dragoman and guide in the locality will not see you go in as you were. Mrs Hailstrom wouldn't have been pleased about that!' The lounging figure straightened.

Leonie swung round to actually face him, saying, 'You know my name. You know about me?'

'My dear Miss Saunders! Surely you are not under the impression that I rescue and take on to my launch any careless young tourist who finds herself involved in this kind of situation? It's Mrs Hailstrom I wish to save from embarrassment.' The tone of his voice had changed. It could have been coming from a prince of this land addressing a peasant.

Now, abruptly, Leonie wasn't embarrassed—she was angry! She said, tartness colouring her tone, 'How was I to know that you allow wild animals and their untrained attendants to roam and gallop along your footpaths? Oh, I acknowledge of course that this country, this city, might not be as well run as the ones I'm accustomed to. But surely one should be able to take a stroll by the river without being knocked flying by intractable beasts.' If her words did not carry the kind of timbre his had done, they still held a cutting bleakness.

'It was a perfectly respectable thing that I did. . .' she was continuing, when suddenly she backed away from him, her tirade trailing off.

The tall, dark, handsome man had taken three steps to enter the bathroom, his entire attitude completely changed—hard, contemptuous, but having within it another nuance Leonie couldn't recognise, he said, 'Respectable or not, as you call it, I take leave to inform you that such a situation would never be allowed to happen to any of our women. To walk alone along an unfrequented riverbank at break of day without either companion or guide would be something they would never be permitted to do!'

Interrupting this uncalled-for—and, to her, unjust reasoning—Leonie almost spat out, 'No, I don't suppose they would. They'd be kept shut in and never allowed out on their own. . .poor things!'

'Oh, no, they are not poor things,' answered a soft, slurred voice. 'But now I will show you what might have happened to you.' Two more steps were taken, two arms reached out, one to go low on her back, bringing her to him, the other to catch and hold in a cruel grip the arm that went out to strike.

Inches away, she saw the fierce anger colouring the dark face, and saw also brilliant pinpoints of light sending green eyes to emerald fire. She pushed desperately, only to find she had acted wrongly. Body was suddenly moulded to body, curves and hollows merging and melting into one fused whole as the big tensile form against her twisted slightly. Then the arm clamping her to him moved even lower, ever more tightly, and she came into him with a gasp.

She knew that head was bending towards her; she felt every contour and muscle of his form through the soft voluminous folds of his garments. She twisted her head despairingly.

The man laughed, and it wasn't a light laugh. It echoed from deep within his throat, and then his lips were on hers. And they were not acting as she had begun to fear they would, in a terrifying, brutal demand. They descended on hers gently, moving softly back and forth. Then they shifted, hesitating for a brief moment at the corner of her mouth before travelling downwards, leaving behind small kisses as they went, like fastening a string of pearls along her throat. They stopped, at the opening of her thin blouse, then began to move back and forth as they had on her lips, first on one side and then on the other.

And unexpectedly, not even desiring it, Leonie felt deep inside her coils of jumping nerves that unwound and unwound, and sent her body without volition arching to meet his.

Abruptly, as if that small action had triggered them both into a new dimension, his searching lips had left the soft white mounds he had been caressing slowly one at a time, and for a moment lifted. She didn't want them to go.

But, expert, experienced, the man's lips had found another location for their kisses, and with arms freed now she reached up to clasp them behind his neck, while returning unrestrainedly the slow, heartbreaking caresses he was showering upon her.

She wasn't being wafted away into oblivion either; she knew what she was doing. . .and she didn't care. Whatever happened, whatever befell her, she knew that this man was the other half of her existence.

She found she was being swung up, and in his arms she lay, her eyes closed, golden hair cascading over the brown enfolding arm. Then those seeking lips descended on her own again, but more heavily now, more demandingly, before shifting to traverse slowly and completely the white exposed throat and breasts.

The man felt the shiver, the shudder, that convulsed her cradled body, and a small triumphant laugh escaped him, and from somewhere far in the back of her mind she heard his muttered words—she didn't understand them, they were in Arabic.

Then suddenly, unbelievably, she found she was being stood down, and this man whose name she didn't even know had turned abruptly from her. She heard the words in Arabic that he was using; she heard a reply in the same language but spoken in an entirely different voice. Then, clipped, forceful, came a response which she knew intuitively was an order. That fact carried through to her, however unknown the language. The man's presence darkened the doorway once again, then he was standing before her.

Across only inches of space they looked at one
another. What could she do or say? she wondered.
She hadn't cared then. She didn't care now. But what
must he think of her? Now, if not before, she had
made come true all the derogatory accusations he had
flung at her.

When he did speak, she was taken by surprise.
'Hussein has found your key. It has been washed.' A
brown, long-fingered hand placed it on the vanity basin
behind her, and then he was looking directly at her
again. At a face pinkly flushed from the storm of
emotion she had just passed through; at eyes darkly
hazed still with desire and passion. He said only, 'I
have to go. Hussein will see you on your way,' and
half turned to do so.

Feeling shattered, abandoned as of no account,
Leonie nevertheless put out an entreating hand. She
stammered, 'I'm sorry, I was the one at fault. . .'

A white-enclosed head was shaken. However, the
man only said, 'I really do have to go.' She watched
him depart, desolated, thinking that this cataclysm
couldn't happen to her life in one short half-hour. But
that it had, and that it would have to be lived with, she
knew.

She collapsed then, slumped against the bench at
her back, her legs feeling like unset jelly beneath her,
aware that they wouldn't hold her upright.

Another figure darkened the doorway, though this
one was not clad in white, even if in an ankle-length
djibbah. It said in English, but very accented English,
'Come, lady.' And as she made no move to obey, he
said again, this time more urgently, 'Come quickly,
lady. Getting late—more people come soon.'

Leonie was aware of the words; she glanced at the

young Arab standing before her. She saw his entreating gaze, so taking a deep sustaining breath, she made herself stand upright.

'Oh, yes, of course,' she told him bitterly. 'I expect your master wouldn't want people to know I'm here.'

'No, lady,' answered the voice in its thick English. 'Not my master. He can do anything! But you. . .'

Oh, yes, she supposed so! This young man's four words said it all. . .especially when remembering about whom he was speaking.

Turning to pick up her key, she saw her reflection in the mirror. 'Good God!' she muttered, thinking of all those Arabs waiting for trade beside the hotel. Mrs Hailstrom would suffer more embarrassment if she, Leonie, was seen walking back through them looking as she did now—dishevelled and muddy might have been better.

Deliberately, she splashed cold water over her flushed face and dried it carefully. Deliberately again, she picked up the comb, but this time used it straight away, not going through the rigmarole she had used when another man had been watching her. Then, hair in place, face even now beginning to get back its normal colour, she swung round and followed the swiftly moving figure before her.

It went up three steps before thrusting out a delaying arm. A full minute went past, and Leonie was beginning to get impatient when she was beckoned forward. Hussein was halfway along the jetty. He threw two words to her as he had done before, and she went. . .quickly.

Past him, and then a few more yards, and she was on the footpath. Right at the very top of it, even now disappearing from sight, were two fully enveloped black-clad women. But the path she made herself

slowly saunter along was empty—for seconds only.
Three female tourists accompanied by their dragoman
were just rounding the corner of the hotel. All they
would see, she thought acidly, was a young girl out for
a pre-breakfast stroll.

CHAPTER THREE

LEONIE gazed over this scene to which her employer had brought her on this their last day in Cairo. Social smile on her face, a young attractive man from the Embassy beside her—she was the very epitome of a carefree young girl enjoying herself.

But, deep inside, all she was aware of, even in these exotic surroundings, was a dark, sculptured, handsome face; a face that she gazed at while having her first cup of tea in the morning, and which was the last thing she saw before going to sleep at night. And which, she knew also, was even now superimposed on the buildings and soaring palm trees all around her.

Oh, well, she thought, this was his country; it wouldn't happen once she returned home. Her attention was brought back to her surroundings by a sharp exclamation. Beside her, Greg said curtly, 'Will you excuse me a minute, Leonie? I must grab His Excellency quickly. He might not have seen who's just come in—they're more than a little late.'

He was swiftly gone, leaving her with the other couple with whom they had been chatting. All three of them looked round, wondering what the flap was about.

Leonie's heart plummeted. It was no good doctors contending that such a thing didn't happen. She knew differently, because that organ was somewhere down near her toes. She fastened more firmly the fingers holding her saucer as the cup it held began to rattle against it.

Five men had entered the pleasant terrace adjoining the garden in which they were standing. Four of them she had seen once before—at an airport. One of them she had seen a second and yes, a third time. Oh, heavens! She knew she must turn away, give her attention to other things, but for her life's sake she couldn't!

The newcomers were being greeted now by Greg, who was escorting them to the Ambassador. She heard her companions speaking, and absently answered a question put to her.

But suddenly she felt the need for protection, and told them, 'I'd better go and see how Mrs Hailstrom is faring.' So she went and stood close to the older woman, who was standing amid a laughing, gesticulating group.

Mrs Hailstrom turned to smile at her, then said sharply, 'You look pale, Leonie. You're not unwell, are you? You haven't been eating or drinking anything you shouldn't have done?'

'Would I dare, after the lecture you read me?' Leonie made herself speak, but she couldn't force herself to smile. Then, not expecting it, definitely not expecting the new arrivals to end up anywhere near them, she found with heart-stopping suddenness that she had been wrong.

The strolling newcomers had come to a halt beside them, and the Ambassador's voice was saying to the Prince, 'Our counterpart and his lady from the French Embassy, Your Highness, and Mrs Hailstrom from Aswan.'

There came a murmur of greetings to the Prince, then the clipped, assured voice of the Ambassador was continuing, 'Major Hasaz, His Highness's aide-de-camp. His Highness the Sheikh Hassan Wallifa, and the Sheikh Ahmed Wallifa.'

Leonie's employer smiled, greeting them all, smiling more warmly at both the Arab Sheikhs. Then she was introducing Leonie. Not wanting this, but knowing she had to go through with it, Leonie resorted to good manners. She half-curtsied to the Prince, said how do you do to the others.

She received a half-smile from the Prince, a small bow from three men, and two words from a familiar soft English voice. 'Miss Saunders!' Then the group was departing, and she would dearly have loved a chair to sink into.

For now she knew that that threaded cord stretching from one entity to another *had* been there—but all she had seen, all that had been visible, was a grave handsome face with hooded green eyes from which no expression whatever had shown.

Mrs Hailstrom was saying to her, 'I think I'll go and say my thank-yous and then we'll leave, Leonie. I've been to that physiotherapist this morning, which, thank goodness, was my last day, so I am a little tired.'

For the older woman to admit tiredness caused Leonie to acquiesce quickly, and in a few short minutes they were in the black limousine, heading back to the hotel.

Leonie would dearly have loved to ask about the two young sheikhs—why the younger one was introduced first and called His Highness, and why the other older and much more authoritative figure was given only the title of Sheikh. She had noticed, of course she had, that the same black and silver cord banded both their kaffiyehs.

But she took note of the tiredness, and yes, even the sign of strain in her employer's face. And, much as she would have liked to ask questions, she kept silent. She gazed, still enchanted, out at the hot, teeming streets of this city of Cairo through which they were driving—a city she hadn't seen nearly enough of, but which she would be leaving in the morning.

And even in their rooms, settling Mrs Hailstrom down for the evening, she didn't bring the matter up. She saw that tablets were placed on the night table. She phoned down for the dinner Mrs Hailstrom had suggested, then, leaving Sunna in attendance, she left for her own room to dress for her own evening.

Finally ready and quite pleased with the result, she made her way next door. 'Come in if it's you, Leonie,' called her employer as she tapped on it.

She went in, thinking that tonight she did look almost beautiful. She waited for comment from Mrs Hailstrom, who was eating her dinner from a small table set beside her chair. She got no comment, but she did receive a large encompassing smile and a raised eyebrow.

'It *is* nice, isn't it?' she asked, pirouetting. The midnight-blue chiffon swirled about her.

'It is indeed,' she was answered. 'One of the top houses' creations, I presume?'

'Oh, no!' Leonie was shocked, then gave a gamine grin. 'But doesn't it look like it? I only took one cocktail dress over from home when I escorted my other patient to England. . .'

'Oh, yes,' interrupted her employer, 'you escorted someone else with a broken leg, didn't you?'

'Yes, and it was that distinguished surgeon you called an old goat who offered me this job. Wouldn't it have been too dreadful if he hadn't? I shouldn't have seen Egypt then. Still, about this dress, I saw it in a shop just off Regent Street, and although falling in love with it I knew I couldn't really afford it. Actually, it was more than I should have paid, but I'd earned a free air ticket from Australia to England and back, so I bought it to take home, wrapped carefully in tissue paper.

'I really don't know what Greg is expecting me to turn up in. I asked him what one wears dining at a top Egyptian nightclub and he said to ask you.' Leonie giggled. 'I wonder what he thinks we wear in Australia?'

'He's a very ambitious young diplomat, and pleasing me is one of many steps up the ladder,' said her employer. 'Now show me.'

Leonie displayed the beautiful dress, which was the colour a clear sky at midnight would show. The high-cut neckline stitched with its outlines of silver glowed and glittered as she moved, and the blue underslip beneath outlined high young breasts. But it was the sleeves that marked it. Sheer, voluminous, they were gathered into a wide band embroidered in zigzag silver. No one could say it was immodest, but its clinging folds left little to the imagination.

'It *is* a beautiful dress. . .but for tonight?' said Mrs Hailstrom slowly, then her tone went crisp, and she said, 'It's lovely, and so are you tonight. Go and enjoy yourself.'

'I will. But I don't think I'm earning that salary you're paying me. My job isn't to go gallivanting around at night enjoying myself.'

'Your job is to be here when I need you, and tonight I don't! Also, Leonie, without you being here with me, I wouldn't be allowed to go home to Aswan, and I simply couldn't bear that—staying in Cairo three more weeks waiting for the final X-rays. So off you go. And you can resume what you call your job in the morning, looking after me on the way home.'

'OK, then.' Leonie sent an all-encompassing glance

over the room, at the half-eaten dinner, at the night table set with its glass of water and tablets laid out ready to be taken, at Sunna.

Her gaze, returning to her employer, encountered a wide stare of malicious comprehension. She felt the colour rise to her face.

'Well. . .' she told the older woman defiantly, 'I was just checking as I'm supposed to do. But I am off now and I'll see you in the morning. Goodnight.'

The door closed behind her with a little snap, she walked down the long corridor, saying a soft good-evening to the porter at his station there. Downstairs, stepping from the lift, she stood gazing across the vast marble foyer. The three other members of tonight's party were standing on the colourful inlaid motif speaking with the hotel manager. In their white dinner-jackets and dark trousers, in the beautiful dress the woman wore, they could have been posing for a stage set.

Greg had turned as she walked towards them. Leonie saw the glance he was bending on her—on all of her—and grinned inside herself. But she still smiled warmly at him as he came to take her arm. Then they were departing, saying goodnight to Mr Hamid as they went.

Outside a big black limousine waited, and their guest went to sit in front beside the chauffeur. Because it seemed that tonight they were to be driven to their destination. Leonie sat starry-eyed, her gaze glued to the busy crowded streets. She *had* been out sight-seeing, with Greg on one ocasion, with Mrs Hailstrom on others, but only to such recognised tourist spots as the Pyramids and the museums and such. She had never been out on the streets at night, and, though there were hundreds of cars speeding all along beside them, this city, with its strange noises, its so different dress, and most of all its colour, brought to her fascinated gaze a scene she had always associated in her mind with the East.

And inside the restaurant, it was just the same; a scene out of the *Arabian Nights*, she thought delightedly. Different entirely from anything she had yet seen. But as she was escorted to their table she wondered at its being only half full.

No, they were the wrong words. Where they had been seated the large room all around was crowded, with tables scattered amid tall marble pillars filled with tourists of both sexes. With Egyptians too, seemingly unaware of the laughing, exclaiming foreign patrons about them as they spoke in low tones with one another. There seemed no Egyptian women present, but she wouldn't know, decided Leonie, if they were in Western dress.

She did wonder for a brief moment why that space opposite them was not occupied, only two of the tables holding patrons, both by two Army officers in full regimentals but with no companions. After all, this was a venue to which one came to enjoy oneself.

She saw Greg lean across and mutter a few words to Henri, his counterpart from the French Embassy who was their dinner guest, and also saw the affirmative reply. Then they were trying to find their way through a strange menu, giving laughing orders and hoping for the best.

Irène, Henri's wife, was tending to monopolise Greg, and, thought Leonie, she could get on with doing just that. Tonight was a scene out of time, that she just wanted to enjoy and remember, which with another episode she would wrap up carefully and take home to Australia.

Greg was leaning across to her, asking as he took in her sparkling eyes, her interest in the people and places surrounding them, 'You like it, don't you, Leonie? You'd make a great diplomat's wife. You enjoy the different localities and their inhabitants. . .all the different sorts of inhabitants. I've noticed it!'

'Oh, yes, I expect I do that, but then I can do that living among ordinary people. Being a diplomat's wife I wouldn't be able to. Now, there's an up-and-coming diplomat's wife,' Leonie gestured towards Irène. 'An Ambassador's niece, no less, brought up to the position.'

'Certainly she is—in all ways. But she. . .oh, well, you pays your money and you makes your choice, as the man says.' Greg flipped a hand and turned to speak to Henri.

Oh, wouldn't she love to be able to have a choice to make? went through Leonie's mind, while she apparently gave all her attention to the pretty girl opposite her. *She* would certainly pay her money and count whatever eventuated from her choice as well worth it. If she only could. . . But with her, she knew she had no choice.

Immersed in her own thoughts, she hadn't been aware of the bustle erupting suddenly behind her, but, noting the veiled interested expressions on the diplomatic faces at her side, Leonie also looked. Moving along a passageway cleared for them came a party. And what a party! It could certainly have emerged from an *Arabian Nights* story. Six men were walking in a group with three others walking beside and behind them. The Army officers seated in that empty section were upright now, standing at their tables as they greeted the newcomers.

Leonie sat rigid. She hadn't expected to see Ahmed this afternoon; she certainly hadn't expected to see him tonight.

The Saudi Prince was being seated in the centre of the longer table, his aide joining the Army officers. But on either side of the Prince were the two members of the Wallifa family. And at the back of those three central figures stood a man behind each chair. Only one, however, behind the prince, was clad in white. The other two were covered in burnouses, striped wide in black and silver. Heavens, in this day and age, bodyguards, no less! went more than a trifle acidly through Leonie's mind.

And then, abruptly, her thoughts weren't acidic or astringent. A gaze from green eyes had swept casually around the scattered assembly. It paused, thought Leonie, for the barest moment on their group before passing on. It had just been the look anyone could have made while settling in at a table, but Leonie knew that that glance had noted them, and she felt a shiver of apprehension stir through her entire body. Though he was probably only about her own age, the aura of this young sheikh of the Wallifa was one of fierceness. . .ruthlessness.

She acknowledged that the other Wallifa sheikh seated there at the same table gave that impression too, but with him it was a controlled ruthlessness. Ahmed didn't have the fierce eagle eyes of his cousin, and he didn't show any interest in the crowded restaurant either. But the young Sheikh Hassan knew they were there, even with only one brief glance. Ahmed, however, was giving his attention entirely to the Prince by his side.

So Leonie brought her attention back to her own party, in time to hear Henri saying, 'It is not supposed to be official, this Saudi visit, but the two other men in white *are* Government officials. . .and those Army officers are high-ranking.'

'Yes,' answered Greg. 'However, I expect this entertainment tonight has been set up for the Prince. I shouldn't imagine that the Wallifa cousins would come to a public place like this for their amusement.'

'No, I don't expect they would, but the Prince will most likely enjoy a crowded nightclub away from his own country. . .' A clash of cymbals interrupted Henri's words, and a group of tumblers bounded on to the round polished dance-space. Food began to be eaten as the act continued.

A little later, waiting for a next course, Leonie turned to Greg and asked, 'Why was the younger man introduced this afternoon before the older one of the same surname? And why was he introduced as "His Highness" while the other one was only given the title of Sheikh?'

'Because Hassan is the heir to the ruler of the Wallifa; and the Wallifa are a very important tribe which everyone tends to keep an eye on. They have oases in the far desert and outside Aswan, and on the Nile next door to the Sudan.' Here Greg allowed his gaze to slide over the far table and its occupants before adding, 'The information we have is that the Sheikh Ahmed's mother is a Greek lady and that his father, the Sheikh Yusef, spends a lot of his time away on business.'

'Oh. . .' was all Leonie found to answer. Having an oasis near Aswan might account for the more than polite greetings between Mrs Hailstrom and the two young Arab sheikhs this afternoon. They could have known one another for a long time.

She dismissed that from her mind. Much more

important to her was the fact that Ahmed had a Greek mother. That might mean that he could have some European concepts as well as Arab ones. But however important to her these thoughts were, she found they had suddenly departed.

The overhead lights had been dimmed, and drums began to play, softly at first, while a spotlight circled the dance space which had been the venue of the other entertainment this night. On to this polished floor glided a woman. . .no, she was only a girl. But she was beautiful. In floating gauze that did nothing to hide the figure it so sparsely covered, she glided to a halt before the long table. She began to dance.

The beating drums sent out their call of anticipation throughout the crowded room—and to not only the Egyptian patrons either. Leonie took her gaze from that twisting, sensuous figure to look about her. Even Greg, the cool diplomat, had a fist clenched on the table, eyes half shut to hide any expression, while on Henri's closed face she saw the glint of moisture.

Every tourist eye was fixed upon that brilliant spotlight and the gyrating form within it, the room about them silent except for the voice of the drums. But suddenly those voices were dwindling slowly to a whisper; that sensuous, exquisite figure bending backwards, allowing every movement of body, of arms, of fingers, to give forth its message.

It was mesmeric, that call to each throbbing sense, and even Leonie felt her own pulse leap running to meet it. Sharply she looked away, shaking her head to clear it. Her glance rose and she saw that one other person in the vast restaurant was also not looking at that spellbinding dancer. Across a crowded smoke-filled room, the brilliant spotlight caught two pinpoints of brightness. Leonie knew that they were green, and that Ahmed Wallifa was looking directly at her.

Dredging up every atom of love, of desire from deep within her, she beamed it across that stretched threaded cord she knew was there between them, and for one long out-of-time moment they looked directly at one another.

Then, with a running sound of drums, a clash of cymbals, that twisting, sensuous form had sunk down prostrate at the Prince's feet. It wasn't he, however, who leaned forward and flung the purse at her down-bent head. It was Hassan, and as the gold spilled out, she gathered it to her, laughing, then springing to her feet she was gone.

Cutlery was taken up to eat food which had been left uneaten on plates. Leonie glanced at hers and, not wanting it, pushed the dish aside. As she did so, she saw a look pass between Greg and Henri. Henri nodded, and Greg raised a hand, beckoning to a waiter.

Henri said, 'I think we will go and have coffee and liqueurs at the Embassy. Things might start to get a bit hectic here any minute now.' And even as he spoke a troupe of Arab dancers began to filter through to the entertainment area.

'Too late,' came Greg's voice, and he added an order for coffee to the bill which he had asked for.

Wondering, Leonie glanced at him, then, as a subdued commotion erupted from further down at the Wallifa tables, she saw that they were beginning to move, to walk through a pathway which waiters made for them. Greg, of course, thought Leonie a trifle maliciously, being the perfect diplomat, would certainly not rise and go before them.

The group in their robes of spotless white passed

only yards from their table. Neither party glanced at one another. And one of them, noticed the girl in the midnight sky dress of blue gazing from beneath downcast lashes, also looked neither to right nor left, but was bending a white-enclosed head courteously to what his elder companion was saying.

It was beginning to get a bit noisy, the noise and music louder. This, now, was a very different kind of entertainment. Eating slowly, Irène said, 'You know, that girl would make her fortune in England. . .and more so in America. She was fantastic!'

Answering somewhat drily, Henri told her, 'She doesn't need to go to those places to make her fortune. She is a very wealthy young lady.'

'But—I know it was gold that was thrown at her. Still, that wouldn't add up to a fortune.' Irène had a furrow between her white brows, clearly working it out.

When Greg replied, his tone carried impatience. 'Oh, that! That was just a gesture from time immemorial. . .an act! Take it from Henri, that dancer is wealthier than probably any of us. Now, finish your coffee and we'll go.' Leonie agreed—it *was* getting noisy.

The bill was paid—no, signed for, she saw. A wad of notes was placed on the table with a gesture to their waiter, then Greg was pulling out Irène's chair, Henri doing the same for Leonie, and they were threading their own way through the close-packed tables—but with no waiters making a path for *them*!

They moved slowly between laughing, gesticulating patrons intent on enjoying themselves, then stood out on the footpath waiting for the car.

And in the limousine large enough to allow room for them all to get on with their own thoughts they drove carefully through streets still crowded with traffic, between footpaths thronged with colour and dress so different from all their own countries. Because tonight, this late, it was mostly Egyptians who were in evidence, not tourists.

Pulling up before the façade of Shepheards, Greg told the others, 'Wait in the car, I'll just see Leonie to the lift and be right back.'

In the event, he wasn't right back. They were held up by an English party who had been at the reception earlier that day. Greg was pleasant, as of course he was bound to be, but, finally extricating himself, he piloted Leonie to the lifts, saying, 'You'll be all right now,' waved a hand in farewell, and was gone.

Watching him depart, Leonie smiled and turned to enter the lift. Like once before in this hotel, if on a very much higher floor, she stopped dead. A long brown hand indicated a way before it, and she stepped past to go in front of the white-clad figure—only to proceed a short distance across the vast marble foyer, up some steps and on to the small balcony which guests used while waiting. Leonie passed an immobile figure in a black and silver burnous facing outwards and who looked straight through the smile she sent to him.

And in a corner, away from the least sight of prying eyes, Ahmed Wallifa said, 'I have to go along to the launch to pick up some papers, and. . .what is the phrase one uses?. . .just stopped by.'

'It might be the phrase ordinary people use. I really don't expect it applies to you,' Leonie smiled at him.

'Well, would the words apply to me if I tell you that I am leaving for Saudi Arabia in a few hours, but first wanted to indulge myself before I go? Indulge myself by discovering if an ice maiden I saw across a crowded restaurant is still an ice maiden close up.'

Leonie gave a gurgle of laughter. 'And is she?' she asked softly.

Those eyes she had often seen hooded were not half shut now. They gleamed as emerald pinpoints of light. Then Ahmed's two hands came to rest on her shoulders before sliding, oh, so slowly, down her arms over the frail ice-blue chiffon. Leonie felt as if every hair on them stood upright. But the tight, firm fingers remained clasped about her wrists, and first one hand and then the other was raised to have a kiss dropped within.

Leonie swayed towards him, but those hands held her firmly away. He was asking her something, her consciousness knew that, but she couldn't take in what it was he was saying. He asked it again, and she knew she replied. One hand released itself, one long brown finger stroked down her cheek, and the soft voice when it spoke in English said, 'I'll see you in a few days.' Then she found herself walking towards the lift, Ahmed on one side of her, Hussein stalking along behind.

This time she did enter the lift. And, walking on air, she also went inside and closed the door of her room behind her, to lean back against the hard wood.

What was that question Ahmed had asked her and that she knew she had answered the second time? Yes, that was it. 'Do you ride?' he had enquired.

Of course she rode, she thought dismissively—if it was horses that Ahmed had meant. She had been brought up among horses. Pushing such an absurd subject from her mind, Leonie reached behind her and pulled the zip of her lovely dress. Stepping out of it, she hung it away in the wardrobe—this dress which Ahmed had said she looked like an ice maiden in.

Leaving the rest of her clothes where they fell, she

pulled on a short cotton nightdress and walked to the window to slide back the curtain. A window opening on to a vast, alien country which already had placed her senses in enthrallment to it.

She went down into oblivion, thinking of the charming Ahmed who had been so different just now from the image her memory bank held of him.

CHAPTER FOUR

'Miss . . .Miss!' From out of the deep sleep into which she had drifted, Leonie shot upright. Sunna was gently shaking her. Dazedly Leonie glanced up at her, rubbing the sleep from her eyes, then abruptly she was out of bed. 'Mrs Hailstrom?' she asked quickly, beginning to drag on the towelling robe lying across the foot of her bed.

'No. . .no! The lady is all right. But she said it is late and we have to go. . .'

Dismissing the words Sunna was saying, Leonie walked quickly from her door and through into the next one. She drew a deep breath of relief. Her employer was reclining in a chair, her gaze on the Nile as she ate her breakfast.

'Heavens, I got a fright!' Leonie exclaimed. 'I suppose I slept in.'

'You haven't really, but it *is* eight o'clock, and we leave the hotel at ten. I thought you'd better have your breakfast and then pack. I've ordered it to be delivered in your room,' said Mrs Hailstrom.

Leonie shook her head, saying, 'I'm not here to be waited on. . .' but was waved impatiently away. So in her own room she ate the breakfast that was there waiting, then dressed in working clothes and, her cases locked, went next door. But she told herself while doing so that she looked a different girl from the one who had stood before a tall white-clad Arab last night, who had been. . . It was her turn now to be impatient, and she pushed away the thought of a lovely blue

47

dress, and of a man who had told her she looked beautiful in it.

From then on she found she had no more time in which to think of Ahmed until they were settled in the small plane and were airborne, and she gazing out of her window to see the city of Cairo, both modern and ancient, slide away beneath her.

Unclipping her seatbelt, she leaned across to ask, 'Are you all right?'

And beside Sunna Mrs Hailstrom looked at her—and smiled. 'Oh, yes, Leonie,' she answered. 'Because, of course, I'm going home.' Leonie smiled at the complete satisfaction showing in the other woman's face, then turned to gaze out of her own window.

Cairo had drifted away, and now the vivid green which had coloured both sides of the river was gone too. They were flying across what seemed just bare brown earth. Except for an occasional huddle of native buildings and, once, what must have been a military camp with countless vehicles scattered about it, there was nothing to break the monotonous brown terrain below.

Then she saw there was something else. There was another plane flying beneath them. It was so far down, just skimming the earth. As she watched, it turned, its every outline brilliantly clear. Then, as their own plane turned too, incredibly she saw that it was only their own shadow.

The journey unfolded. Luxor was left behind, when suddenly, far down beneath, Leonie saw water—a vast lake of it. Next came a cluster of buildings which, judging by their height, must be hotels. Then they were past and making a run over an air-strip.

They were going much too fast, she thought breathlessly. But then came the bump of wheels as they touched down, and they were at their journey's end.

'Oh, good—Rashid!' Mrs Hailstrom was exclaiming as she walked carefully down the steps with Leonie at her shouder. An old man was salaaming before her, and there were wide smiles on both their faces. 'This is Rashid, Leonie. He has always been with us, and with Giles before me. Here's Miss Saunders who has come to help me, Rashid.'

'Miss. . .' Rashid gave another salaam, then pointed to a small stool set beside the high steps of a Land Rover. A question in sharp Arabic from him caused Mrs Hailstrom to laugh, but all she said was, 'Let's get home.'

'Home!' muttered Leonie when they pulled up before the house. She sat staring at it. 'No wonder Greg and his friends angle for invitations!' she told the woman beside her. For this place was beautiful—low, spreading, either washed or painted white, with arches and verandas of scrolled stone everywhere.

And unexpectedly, remembering that she had been told that this was a parched land where it was supposed never to rain, there was the garden! With its palm-trees soaring between the green and dusky pink of blooming oleanders; with its flowering vines climbing against those walls of brilliant white exuding a fragrance that perfumed even the hot, blazing land about them, the place was pure magic.

Leonie faced the older woman, saying carefully, 'I thought you would have no garden at all, and I didn't expect I'd be coming to live in what's almost a palace!'

Watchfully helped to alight, Mrs Hailstrom was looking around complacently before answering. 'Yes, the house is nice, isn't it?' she said in understatement.

'Giles built it for us when he found I didn't want to go home to live, and as he piped water from the river we've always had a garden. Even fresh vegetables. . .and fruit, citrus mostly. Now, how about that!'

They went into the house, and Leonie found the inside as beautiful as its exterior—tiled floors, cream-painted walls set with glowing pictures that caught at the eye, with huge pottery urns safe in their niches which could have come from the times of the Pharaohs. She gave a sigh of delight.

'No wonder you wanted to get home!' she said. 'But for now, would they be able to get you a late lunch, and then, I think, a rest with some tablets? OK?'

'Rashid will have all that organised, but first he must show you your rooms.'

Rooms. . .plural, thought Leonie, moving off after the old man. And that was what she did find—a large high-ceilinged bedroom opening out on to a small veranda, all tiled in a beautiful coloured mosaic. The shower and deep square tub in the bathroom was tiled also, but in plain palest green. It was a place of restfulness yet elegance.

'Whew!' muttered Leonie, going to wash her hands and comb her hair. She felt the same impression all around her as she followed the short corridor to find another Arab, clad in the ubiquitous djibbah, waiting.

'This way, lady,' he told her, and, smiling at this dark stranger, Leonie followed him out to another veranda, a screened one this time, where Mrs Hailstrom was sitting at a round table set for lunch.

'This is Karim, Leonie, Rashid's son. . .one of Rashid's sons,' introduced her employer, smiling at them both.

Saying hello to this man she had already greeted,

Leonie took the seat he was holding out for her. She said, eyeing the food on the table, and on her plate, 'Your whole place is so lovely, Mrs Hailstrom. As I said before, no wonder you wanted to come home!'

'Yes, and that's what I call it—home. I went back to England after the war, to live. . .and to try to have children, but Giles and I weren't granted any, so, his work being here in Egypt where he was liked and wanted, even after independence, we came back.

'Although we had a house in Cairo by then, he built this place because a lot of his work was in the far south of the land, especially in the desert. You know, Leonie, life is funny.' The older woman's voice had slowed, her attention gone from this place, this time. . .

Then she was continuing, 'My sister and I were heiresses, the only remaining family of our grandfather. But, where she was a social butterfly, loving the gay life, enjoying the entertainments of a great city, realising that the first two children she had were a necessary evil, she had three others very much against her wishes. While I, who desperately wanted children, had none. Yes, life *is* strange,' the woman across from her repeated absently. 'But still,' here, the malicious grin she had sent to Greg from the back seat of the car carrying them to their hotel in Cairo surfaced, 'I think I've snared one of those children, one my sister didn't want me to get, who loves out here as much as I do. . .so we'll see.'

Leonie gazed across at the complacent face, shaking her head. She said, 'I think you're a wicked woman, Mrs Hailstrom. Thank goodness all *I* have to do with you is look after your arm. . .and see you don't use it until it's ready to be used. Now, how about a painkiller and a rest?'

'All right, and I suppose I can tell you that my arm is hurting a bit. And I think we'll skip afternoon tea today, because of this,' her arm went out in a throw-away gesture to the table still carrying food from their late meal. 'Now, what would you like to do? Go and look around?'

Leonie laughed. 'I certainly would,' she replied definitely. 'I feel I'll never see enough of it. And that's just here. . .around this house and gardens, never mind out there in the great big yonder.'

'You're a girl after my own heart,' she was told, then she heard, 'Oh, by the way, do you ride?'

She didn't answer. The three words joltingly trans-planting her to a dim, silent foyer, to a man who was leaving her, and who had also uttered those same words; words which had passed over a mind occupied with a far different subject.

'Leonie!'

Abruptly brought back to her surroundings by that sharply uttered name, she answered quickly, 'Oh, sorry. I was trying to take in the meaning of your words. Yes, I do ride. I was brought up on a prop-erty—only a small one, but I rode all kinds of horses, and worked them in all kind of situations! Why?'

'Because I have horses which need exercising—my own, which you wouldn't be able to ride, and three others. I was wondering, if you do ride, would you care to help Mohammed exercise them until I'm well enough?'

'Mrs Hailstrom. . .' Leonie's voice held fright, 'you do know it will be some time before you can ride, don't you?'

'Oh, I suppose so. That's why I'm pleased you can ride. Now, Leonie, can you exercise those horses? I'm afraid poor Mohammed has had rather a lot to do.'

'Too right—I'd love to! But that's not work, and I *am* here for one special reason.'

'Pooh. . .! All right, now that's settled, I think I'll go to bed now.'

Leonie settled her down, then walked along a tiled corridor, expecting it to be the one that led outside. But she soon lost her way.

'These must be guest quarters,' she muttered, eyeing the beautiful palatial suites, and turned, flustered a little, not wanting to be where she shouldn't.

Retracing her footsteps, she found where she had taken the wrong turning, then began on her tour of exploration.

This time of day must be the equivalent to the European siesta, she thought, because no one at all was in evidence working in this exquisitely kept garden. Wandering through herself, she inhaled the fragrance, and even broke off a cluster of carnation-pink oleanders, raising them to her face.

Finding a cobbled path which she thought might lead to the stables, she followed it. Yes, here were the back premises of what was almost a palace, and that building further along looked very much like stables. Making her way to it, she came to an abrupt halt. A man, an Arab, was coming to meet her. He bowed slightly, saying, 'Welcome, lady. You have come to see the horses. I am Mohammed.'

Not knowing how to address him, Leonie just smiled warmly. 'Yes, I've come to see the horses,' she answered, 'if it's all right with you, Mohammed.'

CHAPTER FIVE

Sitting beside the wide river, which wasn't blue at this time of the day, but stained scarlet and crimson, Leonie sighed, knowing she should be going, but lingering for just a few more minutes as the sun sank even lower towards the edge of the world.

Patting the muscled shoulder beneath her knee, she smiled wickedly. This was Mrs Hailstrom's horse she was riding, despite her words to the contrary. But it was an Arab, lighter and more delicate than the heavier, larger animals which were bred in the West.

Irritated, she turned away to her right. The river-bank was empty; there was no need for another rider to come crowding so close.

'There was a time,' said a soft voice in English, 'when you didn't try to move away from me!'

Startled, she turned violently, her horse sidling restlessly as her hands holding the reins tightened. A man was there—an almost stranger, dressed in fawn whipcord breeches, highly polished riding boots, and a white shirt opening on a strong brown throat. Oh, of course, she thought acidly, the shirt that moulded the form it clad would be of silk!

They gazed at one another; the tall, dark, classically handsome man, and the young fair girl, both sitting their horses on the bank of a famous river. He didn't look Arab, thought Leonie. He *did* look Greek. And then her thoughts added, But like a Greek from ancient times.

As he remained silent after those first words, just

allowing his glance to slide over her, over all of her, she said carefully, 'He's beautiful!'

A low chuckle escaped the man—the very first time she had heard him laugh normally. She decided astringently that he wouldn't have laughed like that if she had actually said what she had been thinking. That they were both beautiful.

Then Ahmed was answering her. 'Yes, he is, isn't he?' as he patted the shining black satin coat beneath him. 'This beauty is one of the reasons that the Prince was over here, to look over a colt he has just sired. . .and who is as beautiful as his father.'

'Oh, do you breed horses? I mean, more than one or two to ride?'

Again a low laugh echoed, but this time Ahmed's whole body shook. 'Oh, yes, I think you could say that we breed horses. We are, after all, the Wallifa.'

'Do your. . .' What was she to call them? 'Do your people breed them?'

'Of course, Leonie. I thought you would know. . . What's the matter?' The last words were uttered sharply.

They passed over Leonie. She sat there, and it was her eyelids which had fallen shut this time. Ahmed said again, just as curtly, 'What is it?'

It was the way he had spoken her name, of course, the naturalness of it sending tremors rippling through her entire body. She straightened in the saddle, saying, 'No, I didn't know! How would I?'

'I would have expected you to have asked questions. Mrs Hailstrom could have told you.'

'As far as you're concerned, Ahmed, I don't ask questions. How could I let anyone be aware that I know you? You gave me no incentive to do that. Every time. . .the few times I've met you, been with you, you've always been in such a hurry—and gone.'

'Yes, well, I was escorting the Prince, and I'm afraid everything concerning that time was a formal occasion.'

'It looked like it. . .and so did you! But now you look very different.'

'I expect I do. However, allow me to inform you that these also are dressing-up clothes, as were those others I was wearing in Cairo. My. . .my uncle expects the prestige of the Wallifa to be upheld at all times. But you should see me when I'm in my working clothes, filthy and caked with dust.'

'Truly, Ahmed,' warmth coloured her words, 'seeing you as I've done, I simply couldn't imagine you'd get one dirty mark on you! What work do you do?'

'We breed horses. . .and camels. And believe me, we work while doing it.'

'Was that why. . .?' Leonie stopped speaking, then made herself continue, 'Was that why you asked me if I could ride? Those words passed over me at the time, but I've thought of them since.'

'You probably had other concerns taking up your attention at that particular time,' said Ahmed with amusement threaded through his voice.

Her glance went across to look directly at him, and she felt a burning wash of heat colour her cheeks. Oh, yes, she *had* had other concerns taking up her attention at that particular time!

Then, as if not seeing her reaction to his words, Ahmed was saying, 'I'm expected at the house; we'd better go.'

'Yes.' Leonie glanced round for Mohammed. He always rode with her when exercising the horses. He was there—a little apart from three other riders. Somehow, not even expecting it, she saw that they were wearing the black and white striped burnous she had seen once before across a crowded restaurant, with a black and silver cord to bind their headdress. That piece of attire she had seen on more than one occasion, even if it had been a trifle more elaborate.

'Three attendants,' she said with a raised eyebrow.

From his greater height Ahmed glanced down at her and grinned. She would never have expected to see such an expression on that austere, proud countenance. Unconsciously, she sent the same kind of smile back.

'Yes, well. . .' Ahmed said the same two words he had uttered once before this evening, 'the prestige of the Wallifa, you understand.'

'And how many attendants would that other young man have, the one they called "His Highness"?' Unconsciously, Leonie's voice had adopted more than a touch of irony. It *was* too much to have what amounted to a bodyguard.

'Oh, Hassan would have the same number.'

If he had heard that nuance in her tone, it was clear Ahmed didn't care. It made her say crossly, 'But you're not in the desert now. Surely you wouldn't be frightened that there was any danger here?'

Those strong brown hands must have given directions; the beautiful black stallion broke its easy gait as Ahmed swung round, facing her. She thought, apprehensive suddenly, that his face carried the same expression it had held when he first spoke to her on the launch—scowling, hard, contemptuous.

'Frightened. . .' he said. 'Don't be stupid, Leonie! No one would dare lay a hand on anyone belonging to the Wallifa. . .not even on any of their possessions!

I've told you, it's merely a matter of prestige!' This time—also from directions those hands must have given—his mount lengthened its stride.

They rode now in silence away from a river that showed only the mundane colour of pewter as the water flowed on its way, but remembering Ahmed saying that he was expected at a house, Leonie wondered. Apart from the palatial tourist hotels, and a village, there were not many large houses in Aswan.

'You said,' she remarked carefully, breaking the silence between them, 'that you were expected. Would it be at Mrs Hailstrom's?'

'Where else? Don't tell me you weren't aware that she knows us?'

'I *am* telling you that! How could I be aware of such a thing?'

'I would have imagined you might have been told. Our acquaintanceship is a well-known story.'

'Oh, would you! Well, allow me to inform you that I wasn't told. I don't expect it would occur to my employer to tell me. As far as she's concerned, I met you once at an Embassy reception. She probably wouldn't even remember.'

For once Leonie was angry with him, for once she didn't feel like collapsing into his arms, and tartness showed clearly in her voice.

'Well, that will have to be remedied, won't it? But for now there are more important things to occupy our attention—one of them being. . .' The words broke off for a moment before he resumed, 'I have been away for ten days; have I been in your thoughts at all during that time?'

What **a** question to ask! What was she to say? She did say, 'I expect—after that time we were together—

that yes, you could say you were in my thoughts some of the time.'

Sharp words in Arabic came to her as he turned, his mount again breaking its easy stride. Then he spoke one word softly in English. 'Leonie. . .'

That one word, the way he spoke her name, sent her heart plummeting, and she capitulated completely. 'Of course I thought about you—all the time,' she told him.

She saw the white silk of his shirt rise and fall abruptly, then he was saying, 'Thank Allah for that! A man needs to have some self-respect. Because, even when discussing business, even when among the horses, and most of all when being entertained, your face was before me when it shouldn't have been—and allow *me* to inform you, I didn't like it. I like being always in control of everything remotely concerning me.'

'Did it come even between you and the dancing girls?' she couldn't resist asking.

Ahmed laughed, naturally and out loud. 'Even between me and the dancing girls,' he replied. 'But then I have had to learn my lessons in diplomacy.'

Leonie couldn't answer, she could only remember. Did those words imply what she hoped they did? However, she wasn't to know immediately. They were home, riding through the gates, and their escort had closed up with them as they sent their mounts along the cobbled path to the stables.

Then before she could manage to speak, one of the outriders had dropped to the ground and Hussein was past her and holding Ahmed's stirrup.

'Some more of that prestige,' she muttered, preparing to dismount by herself. Because anyone less likely than Ahmed to need help in anything to do with horses, she couldn't imagine. Then she found, in her turn, someone waiting to help. She gazed down into the dark, handsome face; she put her own hand into the one held out for her, and kicking a foot free, jumped.

Ahmed allowed that hand to drop immediately, and indicated that she go before him. She sent a smile Hussein's way, and got back the smallest bow in return. Then, with a sharp sentence in Arabic to the elderly, bearded man still remaining so straight in the saddle, Ahmed indicated that Leonie precede him.

She asked, her mind still on the horses, 'What do you call him, Ahmed?'

He knew instantly what was the question she was asking. His face slanted down at her carried a wicked grin. 'I had no say in his name. He was called Shaitan before he was ever broken in. And that name was appropriate. He *was* a devil.'

'Oh!' was all she could find to answer. But she could well imagine that breaking in. She did say, 'I suppose it's senseless to ask if it was you who did the breaking in?'

'I should imagine it is. No one else has ever ridden him. Shaitan belongs only to me.'

Dusk was now taking over and before long it would be full dark. Casting a brief glance at the man walking so silently beside her, Leonie thought unhappily that, dressed as he was, incredibly handsome as he was, he belonged to those pictures one saw gazing out from the Sunday supplements, while she. . .unconsciously she sighed.

Thinking such thoughts, she put up a hand to pull off the hat Mrs Hailstrom had insisted she wore up here, pushing back the fair dishevelled hair from her forehead.

'What is the matter, Leonie? What is worrying you?'

Startled, for the second time she heard those words from him, and made herself answer. 'Nothing's the matter. Why should you think that?'

'I think it because it is so. And with you, it is not only a matter of catching your expression; it comes also from the feeling that lies between us.'

Leonie ignored his last words for a moment, deciding to put them away until she could examine them more properly, and told him a trifle acidly, 'If you must know, I was thinking that if it had been now that you'd met me for the first time, ungroomed, with a shiny face innocent of make-up, this attraction between us—because it's there, as you say—might not have taken place. Oh, of course it would have with me. But with you. . .'

Swung round a corner of the house, out of sight of both stables and the wide arched veranda used as a gathering place before meals, Ahmed reached out a hand to grip her forearm. Unconsciously, Leonie's own hand went up to cover it as she felt the tremor that clasp sent to her every nerve-end.

But that emotion didn't seem to extend to her companion. His head came down towards her and she saw in the dimness that he was smiling; a natural smile with no undercurrents at all shadowing it.

'It wouldn't have mattered what you looked like,' that soft English voice was telling her. 'Either looking like a proper young lady ready for a day's work walking on a river footpath. . .or so exquisite in a blue evening dress that I stole time from a business I could ill afford just to come to you. But all that was irrelevant; the damage was already done. *That* happened across a crowded room full of people in a busy airport. . .

'It happened there, that something I had been looking for all my adult life and had begun to imagine I would never find.'

'You didn't even look at me at the airport! You looked at the empty space I could have been.'

'What would you have expected me to do, with all the world and his dog looking on? As were my Prince and your escort sizing up everything with a cold assessing eye. It was a thunderbolt which had come my way, with its lightning striking unexpectedly after it.

'I didn't know who you were—and, more importantly to me, *what* you were! You could have been an. . .an appendage of young Coughlan's. And I wanted to know if that—or anything like it—was on the cards. Well, I knew everything by nightfall. I know all about you.'

'How could you have? You didn't even have a name to start from.'

'Oh, yes, I could. . .and I did!' Ahmed laughed, a low amused chuckle. Then with a throwaway gesture dismissing her words, he said, 'So to me, this evening, dressed as you are, looking dishevelled from riding as you do, doesn't matter. However, other things do.'

He was continuing slowly, as if picking his words, 'We, the Wallifa, Leonie, are not Egyptians. We are Arabs. . .and desert Arabs at that. Our women don't go veiled. Still, while informing you of that, I must yet emphasise that the Arab male is the master of his household. . .and also the master of his women.'

Leonie didn't like the sound of that at all. Her lips set mutinously. Observing it, Ahmed laughed. He told her, 'And with all that said, don't you think that most women—in most circumstances—know how to get their own way?'

Her expression set hard for a moment, Leonie looked up at him. And then she knew that, although there could be customs she might not like, yet in those two outflung brown hands lay all the magic that gave her life its meaning. She smiled radiantly at him.

As he saw that smile, the expression on Ahmed's face changed too. He had swung round and with his back to her, was looking out across a river that was only just discernible now. Leonie gazed at that hard unyielding back, and wondered miserably what she had said. . .had done.

Then Ahmed had swung round again and was saying in his usual voice, 'We had better go in. We are late.' As before, he didn't take her arm, just walked along beside her, two paces distant.

Two women were seated on the wide stone veranda, and her companion moved a step before her, bending to take Mrs Hailstrom's hand. He said pleasantly, 'Good evening, Miss Ferguson,' to the teacher who taught at the girls' school which Leonie's employer had set up.

'You have met Leonie, I see, Ahmed,' stated Mrs Hailstrom.

'Looking at the river at sunset, yes. But I had met her before at the Embassy party, you will remember,' Ahmed replied casually.

Oh, I wish I could dissemble like you, Ahmed! thought Leonie, as she went to stand against the wall until she could interrupt these pleasantries; for now her companion of a few moments ago was being asked, 'Will you have a drink now, or shower and change first, Ahmed?'

'I'll have a drink first—a long one. I have been in the saddle all afternoon! My usual, Karim.'

But Karim was already on his way. He was carrying

two tall glasses on a silver tray, with a slice of lime straddling each rim.

Leonie smiled to herself as the servant went first to offer the drink to Ahmed, then came across to her. Of course that would be the natural thing to do in this country.

She didn't begin to drink. She said, 'I'll go and shower now, Mrs Hailstrom. I had to exercise one of the mares as well as Tarot today, so I'm a little saddle-dirty too. *Ciao!*'

Turning quickly, she walked through the archway into the house. But inside her room, leaning against the door at her back, she put down her drink abruptly, looking at it. Consisting of lime juice, ice and soda, it was just the drink for this country, and Mrs Hailstrom and Gertrude Ferguson always drank it before lunch and dinner. But there was a difference. They had gin added to theirs.

Did Karim add it to Ahmed's too? She wished she knew. If he only drank it like hers, innocent of alcohol, would it mean that he was a strict Muslim? Was he? She wished she knew. . .especially after the things he had said to her only minutes ago, but could she take hope in the fact that he was half Greek?

So, as she had said at other crossroads in her life, she would take each day as it came; for now she supposed showering was the thing to do at this particular time of this particular day, and then go out and meet again this very different Ahmed, the one in modern clothes.

As she walked across the cool tiled floor to the bathroom, shedding her clothes as she went, she felt the astonishment of Ahmed actually coming here. . .and more outstandingly of his coming to this house—to actually stay, as it seemed he was doing.

She had seen how the young Sheikh Hassan greeted her employer, but Ahmed had, until a moment ago, only barely nodded his head. And, too, he knew Gertrude Ferguson. . .

Suddenly, quickly, she reached in to turn on the shower taps. Thinking and wondering would get her nowhere. She stood under the streaming warm water.

CHAPTER SIX

FOR the second time that evening, Leonie went into her bedroom and, shutting the door, leaned back against it.

Earlier she had dressed in another new dress which she also bought in London to take home. In buttercup-yellow cotton, it was a throwback to the fashions of the sixties. Waist pulled in tightly, skirt flaring out to below her knees with a wide band of white at the hemline, it was finished off with a low-cut V-neckline and small extended sleeves.

She had thought she looked attractive, and that the golden yellow suited her, and had hoped someone else would think so too.

But actually, Ahmed had barely looked at her across the polished table—except, of course, when conversation came her way, and politeness made it necessary to do so.

Oh, yes, politeness and good manners were an integral part of his behaviour. Like his soft voice when there was no need for it to carry other tones. However, she had been made aware of a different timbre it *could* assume. . .hadn't she just!

The meal finished, they drank coffee out on the veranda, and it was then that Ahmed had mentioned that he was partly in Aswan to meet his aunt and cousin from Greece.

'Is Helen coming over? Is it to see your father?' exclaimed Mrs Hailstrom, and, listening to that tone, Leonie had wondered what had caused it to surface.

'Helena has had a bad dose of flu. Aunt Helen saw Father when he was away, and he invited them to come to Aswan for a few days and then out to the Middle Oasis when he comes home. He returns on Saturday,' answered Ahmed in his usual soft voice, but was there another nuance beneath it?

He had changed the subject then, saying to Mrs Hailstrom, 'You will have to see the new colt. He is a beautiful thing to behold.'

'It's not only that I'll have to, Ahmed. I'm going to, one way or another! And if there's going to be a trip out to the Middle Oasis, I'm including myself in that as well.'

'But, Mrs Hailstrom, you can't! If you hurt or knock that arm before it's set properly you'll be in trouble. You have a week yet before you go down to Cairo for your X-rays, you know,' said Leonie sharply.

'Oh, phooey! Do you think I don't know how my arm is? Ahmed will just have to make me comfortable, that's all.'

Ahmed laughed, not in the low, amused way she remembered, but out loud, before he answered. 'If I know you, you won't wait for me to make you comfortable. . .you'll see to everything yourself. You forget I've known you for practically always, and am aware of the things you do to get your own way. But I'm still conscious that things will need a little contriving—in all sorts of different ways.'

Maybe things might need some contriving, thought Leonie, aware as she was of how her employer did only what she wanted to do. But hearing that tone in which those last words of Ahmed's had been spoken, she knew without the least shadow of doubt that if there was any conflict, any need to change plans, it would be Ahmed's will that would prevail.

He was saying now, 'If you will excuse me, Mrs Hailstrom, I shall go now. I have some business to attend to before I turn in. Goodnight.' It was a general goodnight to all three of them—and all three of them watched the tall lithe figure clad in the cream linen suit, until it disappeared.

'I expect we can also call it a night, as I have to do my blessed exercises before I follow Ahmed's example and turn in,' said Mrs Hailstrom, and her voice sounded tired.

Rising, with Gertrude moving off the veranda to go to her own house some little distance away, Leonie hurried to the older woman's side, concerned. It wasn't like her to admit tiredness, even in her voice.

But, exercises finished, tablets taken, Sunna in attendance, Mrs Hailstrom seemed to be back to her normal unshakeable self. So after being told for the second time by Mrs Hailstrom not to fuss, that she had probably only herself to blame getting in and out of the Land Rover too much as she went to inspect the school, Leonie raised a hand in goodnight and departed.

Sighing now, she stood away from the door, and walking across switched on only the bedside lamp to undress by. Knowing that she was restless, that sleep was a million miles away, she stood before the dressing-table brushing her hair. At least that was a familiar action among all these other not so familiar ones.

Then, throwing down the hairbrush, she opened the slatted door which the maid had closed when tidying up the room for the night. Before she had taken two steps she smelt the smoke. . .then saw the gleaming arch as a burning object was flung skywards at the opening of her door.

'What are you doing here, Ahmed. . .?' she began,

then, her hand flying to her mouth, she changed the words. 'I didn't actually mean that. I meant, why are you here?'

'Don't get yourself more involved, Leonie. It is just that I have been waiting for you, and thought you would sleep with your doors open. I only want to talk with you.'

Ahmed was sitting crosswise on the broad stone parapet which enclosed the veranda waist-high. He swung his legs round as he was speaking to lounge against it on the inside.

'I'll get a gown, Ahmed,' Leonie told him, turning.

'There's no need. I have no ulterior motive. I am here purely for a discussion about arrangements. You know. . .' Ahmed's words paused for a moment, then carried on as he repeated, 'You know that I have to entertain an aunt and cousin for a few days. . .'

'The lady you call your Aunt Helen is not actually your aunt, is she, Ahmed?' interposed Leonie, not even thinking of what she was saying, thinking only of the man so close to her. He could say what he liked about tonight, or about that night in Cairo, but she could think her own thoughts.

'Oh, has there been a discussion session going on?' said a voice that was not soft at all.

Angry in her turn, Leonie replied just as curtly, 'No, there has not been a discussion session. I never mention you. I have never mentioned you. You're not something or someone I talk about. However, Mrs Hailstrom appears not to like Mrs Paulus. She spoke about her while doing her exercises tonight. She mentioned that she knew her when she used to visit your. . .your mother.'

'Yes—well, Aunt Helen is not actually my aunt. She

was my mother's first cousin and they were brought up as sisters. . .'

Leonie was not interested in this explanation. Unhappily remembering her employer's words tonight that it was such a distant relationship that it could allow marriage between Ahmed and Helena, she had gone on to wonder if that was the reason for this visit.

Because Helena was beautiful and was everything Ahmed could need in a bride—except for not being an Arab. Malleable in all ways to his wishes, aware from birth that she would be expected to go where her husband was, and endowed with a face and body no man would tire of looking at.

Then of course for her was the fact that Ahmed was wealthy enough to take her everywhere, shower her with everything her soul could want.

'Is he wealthy?' she had asked quietly. She knew he had that launch. She knew he dressed expensively, but after all he was only a desert Arab, and she hadn't thought they were wealthy as such.

Mrs Hailstrom had stopped speaking and swung round to look at her. She had seen only polite interest on the young face. She had said, 'Yes, he is. Very wealthy!'

Ahmed was interrupting those thoughts, saying, 'But I didn't wait here where I actually should not be to talk about relations, whether close or otherwise. At least, not in that sense. I wondered if you—and Mrs Hailstrom, of course—would care to come for a picnic tomorrow; to the islands in the river.'

Leonie stayed still and silent for a long minute, hugging these words to her. It was long enough for Ahmed to say, 'Forget it, Leonie. I only thought you would like to go and see them. You haven't been yet!'

'Ahmed, I would like that above everything—to go

out with you as if on an ordinary picnic. Even in my imagination I didn't think of that. But how do you know I haven't been? Because I *have* heard of them.'

'I know! Now if, as you say, you would care for this outing, I had better make some arrangements.' Ahmed leaned back indolently against the parapet—this so different Ahmed, so that Leonie gave a little jump and sat on it, although quite some distance from him.

She wriggled her bare feet in ecstasy. Just to be sitting here with Ahmed making arrangements for an ordinary picnic, as one did in an ordinary practical life, was happiness enough. She asked, 'Where do we go, and who's going?'

'I thought we would sail the Nile in a felucca for a short hour or so, then go over to Elephantine Island to see the Aga Khan's Mausoleum. It is a tourist thing that people go to. Then we could lunch in the gardens of Lord Kitchener.'

'I've heard of them, Ahmed. Fancy Lord Kitchener creating so much beauty, being also the great soldier that he was. They're quite famous, aren't they?'

'Yes, they are. But Egypt lays its hand on all kinds of people, Leonie.' Ahmed was looking past her into the vast empty starlit outside as he spoke. 'It happens in many cases. Also the desert too exerts its own kind of spell.'

Remaining silent for a long minute, Leonie knew that for her too the spell of Egypt had laid itself on her. It caused her to ask, even if a trifle hesitantly, 'What does your family consist of, Ahmed? I do know you have a father, and. . .'

'Yes, I have a father and stepmother, and two young sisters who are away at school in England.'

'Oh, I thought that maybe only the sons of families here went away to school—if anyone does go away.'

Ahmed was laughing down at her. 'Are these questions a way of trying to get a certain type of information from me? Because yes, that does apply in most cases. Still, times are changing, here as well as in the West, even if a little more slowly—the exception to that rule, of course, being my uncle. He will never change.

'When we go to the Middle Oasis,' he went on, 'you will meet old Mr Percival. My father picked him up in Cairo, down and out, and brought him back home. It was from him that I first learnt to speak English—from babyhood until I went away to school. And he has taught succeeding generations of us from then on. Is that some of the information you were trying to dredge up?'

'Yes, that's some of it. I was also wondering how to fix your drink if I had to some time—in the unlikely event that there were no servants around.' Leonie was speaking warily now. 'Do you, for instance, take gin in your lime and soda?' Her breath went in. . .and she held it there.

Ahmed bent down, doubled up. It might have been silent laughter that was shaking that big, lithe body, but it *was* laughter. 'I think maybe,' he told her, still laughing, 'that is one little secret that I intend to keep.'

Had he known what she meant by that question? she wondered. Then she told herself not to be more foolish than she had to be. Being Ahmed, of course he would know. From her experience of him, he knew everything—everything that would or did concern himself. And they hadn't drunk wine at dinner, but then they didn't always. It depended on what they were eating. Oh, well. . .

She glanced up at the silent man beside her, and slid off the parapet, laughing herself this time. 'You know,

Ahmed,' she said, 'I asked Greg what one wore to an Egyptian nightclub. Do I ask you what one wears when going sailing in a felucca on the Nile? Tourists do wear trouser suits here, but Mrs Hailstrom doesn't like me to except for jeans and a big shirt when riding.'

'I accept that, but you are living among Arabs up here. Tomorrow you will be with Europeans—except for me. And speaking of me, it's time I was off.' Ahmed reached for her hand before beginning to slide his length over the guarding wall. And suddenly, no matter what he had said, static was abruptly electrifying their two motionless figures. Hands clasped, tension a threaded cord between them, Leonie yet forced herself to remain immobile.

She had been the one at fault that night in Cairo; she was not going to be tonight. Then that hand, iron-hard, was drawing her forward and she was being cradled against him. Not kissed. . .just held! So they stood, fused together, soft curves melting completely into the tense, strong body.

Ahmed said, 'Leonie. . .'

She stood back, and his arms loosened until she lay within their circle, gazing up at him. It was she now who spoke a name, and it carried a gift if he cared to take it.

'Ahmed!'

'No!' That one word refused it.

For a long moment only silence surrounded the two immobile figures. Then Ahmed said, 'There are too many problems concerning us that have to be straightened out and considered, Leonie. So tomorrow we will go on this picnic of ours, to entertain and be entertained—and later we will see how the Middle Oasis affects you.'

'How does the Middle Oasis affect Helena?' asked

Leonie, leaning further back against those strong enfolding arms.

'That too we will have to find out, won't we?' Ahmed was answering in his easy pleasant tone.

'I suppose we will.' Suddenly angry with him for seeming not to want her, she made to swing out of his arms and turn carelessly away, but she found that what she had thought was iron-hard before was now so in reality. The arms about her were suddenly so tightly crushing as to be hurting.

'Don't play games with me, Leonie,' said Ahmed in a voice which was unexpectedly neither easy nor pleasant. 'Do you think I don't want to carry you in there and make love to you. . .properly, completely? Don't you realise that at other times when offered. . .what you just offered, I have never had to say no? So for now, this time. . .' Her hand was taken again and she felt his thumb roving smoothly up and down its palm. . .and for the second time that night she shivered.

But then he had dropped it and had swung his body over the stone parapet. He said from its other side, 'I'm off now, Leonie. I'll see you at breakfast.'

'Breakfast?' She repeated the one word blankly as if it was an unknown word from another planet. She had never associated Ahmed with anything so mundane as breakfast.

'Of course.' Her companion's tone had turned crisp. 'You do eat breakfast, don't you? And I am staying here in this house, so I imagine I'll be having that meal with you. Or. . .' Suddenly another nuance was being carried in that soft voice which sounded to her like deep amusement. 'Or,' Ahmed was repeating, 'would you care to exercise the horses before that meal I just mentioned, and see the sun come up over the romantic Nile?'

'Oh, Ahmed!' Unable to prevent herself, Leonie interrupted. 'Oh, yes,' she said. 'Could I, with you? I do exercise them sometimes in the morning, but mostly Mohammed and I ride them in the evening.'

'Very well, we'll exercise them all in the morning. I'll have you woken. Now I really must go, or it will be morning before I even get to bed.' A dark hand was flipped, a figure departed. Straining her eyes, Leonie couldn't see him go; he had melted into the night without leaving the smallest shadow, without leaving behind the smallest sound.

It wasn't fair, she thought somewhat acidly. He was an Arab, not a Red Indian. He shouldn't have their abilities as well as his own!

She stood there under this strange Eastern sky with its brilliant shining stars so different from the ones she had looked at so often at home. Here, there was no familiar Southern Cross. Suddenly she shivered and wrapped both arms around herself. Had that action been only because she was cold, or, as the old saying went, had someone just walked over her grave?

Annoyed with herself, she pushed such thoughts away and, turning, made her way inside, where she climbed into bed and pulled up the covers.

Then, light switched off, she turned her face to the window, gazing to where she had stood with Ahmed a few minutes ago. Restlessly she turned, and decided that if she was to be up before dawn she had better try to sleep—and not dream of Ahmed either.

CHAPTER SEVEN

THE next thing she knew was the maid Fathia shaking her gently. 'The lord Ahmed said it is time to rise, lady,' she was saying.

For the first time since she had known his name, Leonie didn't feel that tense jumping of her pulse when she heard it. Still deeply caught up in the unconsciousness of sleep which had been with her for so little time, she said fuzzily, 'What is it, Fathia? What did you say?'

'The Lord Ahmed said only ten minutes. He is waiting. . .' A touch of apprehension coloured the gentle tones of the maid. And abruptly, unexpectedly, the words registered. Last night was all about her. She flung out of bed, making for the bathroom, saying, 'Yes, all right, Fathia, I'll be ready.'

Face splashed with cold water, teeth brushed, she was back in the bedroom in a minute flat. Pants and bra and ankle-length desert boots which she had taken to England with her pulled on, she wondered what to wear? The jeans of yesterday had of course been taken away to wash; no one had expected her to need them this morning so early. She took down a pair of fawn trousers and, shaking her head at the brief tops hanging there and remembering with whom she was riding this morning, she pulled open a drawer. . .and grinned.

Mostly she wore shortie nightdresses at home. But going away for one weekend with a party she had decided, as she had done here, that when in Rome do as the Romans do, and had bought herself the latest in feminine night-wear, fashioned like a man's shirt in dark orange, rounded at the hemline both back and front and slit up the sides to the upper thighs. She muttered as she slid it over her head, still grinning, 'Just the thing!' Ahmed wouldn't know what this was that covered her so completely and loosely.

Of course he wouldn't recognise it, went the astringent thought through her mind. If he—when he—saw a female in night attire, she would most likely be wearing frothy lace and crêpe de Chine.

Strapping her watch to her wrist, she saw she had three minutes left. Then, hair combed, her employer's hat slung round her neck by its thong, she caught up a cardigan, tying it round her shoulders by the sleeves.

'Help, what do I look like?' she muttered again to herself, then decided acidly that she looked like a modern girl, dressed in any old clothes as long as they were the things to wear.

Silently in soft boots, she walked down the tiled hall, and in the dim entrance stood motionless, gazing out at the tall figure waiting for her. Ahmed was leaning indolently against the stone parapet, tapping his polished riding boots with the small flat-ended whip he carried. She might be dressed in modern gear, but as she looked out at him abruptly there was nothing modern at all about her. Her bones melted.

In breeches and boots as he had been yesterday, the white rollnecked cashmere sweater instead of the silk shirt was the only change; but it wasn't fair, she thought, to look as he always looked, no matter what different clothes he wore. Then she found herself looking across the space between them into green eyes. He had turned unexpectedly.

Then, sharply, she wasn't gazing into gleaming emerald pinpoints; his lids had fallen shut.

'Ready?' That easy pleasant voice reached across to her and, making an endeavour to speak the same way, she answered only, 'Yes.'

Ahmed straightened from his leaning position, his eyes opened wide again, looking her over. 'Yes, I see you are,' he said, and deep amusement coloured his words.

Astringency sounded in her own as she replied, 'Well, I haven't got a wardrobe full of clothes wherever I go. And this is the nearest to what Mrs Hailstrom told me I should wear.'

'And very nice too,' was all Ahmed answered from a face that held only seriousness. He reached out a hand and, with his fingers holding her elbow, guided her down the steps and along the little path.

'What is it?' he asked then. 'It doesn't look like a blouse or any top I have seen worn before.'

'I don't suppose you have. It's a nightshirt.' There, make what you can out of that! she thought.

'Good heavens! Do females even wear nightshirts now? That was once a man's prerogative.'

'It may have been once in the dim dark ages. But I take leave to inform you that this is one of the latest items in feminine attire.'

'Well, allow me to take leave to inform you also that yours mightily becomes you.' He might have been paying her a compliment, but his guiding hand had dropped, and Leonie saw why. They had rounded a corner of the house and they were being waited for.

Mrs Hailstrom's horses were there, with the beautiful black stallion called Shaitan that belonged to her companion. His three men were there too. Saying a careful good morning to the space about her, Leonie went over to Tarot. Ahmed moved to take the reins from Mohammed and hold her stirrup.

Unable to prevent herself, she grinned satirically up at him, and, realising what that raking smile meant, the man said, 'He is fresh this morning, and you shouldn't be riding a stallion anyway.'

Leonie just took hold of the reins, placed her foot in the stirrup being held for her and swung up. She gentled Tarot with voice and patting hand, while finding her other stirrup, then had time to glance about her.

Hussein had gone to stand beside Ahmed's stirrup, and Leonie grinned again. More prestige. . .or in this case probably homage, she decided.

Following the sidling, jumping progress of Shaitan just ahead of her, she tightened her reins when Ahmed paused beside the older, bearded Arab. 'This is Ali,' he said. 'The Lady Leonie, Ali.'

The upright, fierce-looking figure raised a hand to his forehead and spoke sharply in Arabic.

Ahmed laughed, then said over a shoulder as he gave his mount a lighter rein, 'Now, show me if you can ride or not, Leonie.'

They were through the gates, and Leonie found herself going a way she had not ridden before, towards wilder, more sparsely inhabited country. Oh, well, she told herself, using Ahmed's words, I've been told no one would dare touch us.

So, following that beautiful collection of gleaming muscles always just in front of her, she gave herself up to flying through the wings of the morning. . . She and Ahmed, and his three. . .bodyguards.

They must have been riding into the east, because the horizon before them was giving up its pearly haze and turning to a faint pink. Ahmed pulled his mount

abruptly to a sliding stop, Tarot going past before she
could stop him. Her companion said,

'Look, Leonie!'

In seconds, crimson and scarlet stained the edge of
the world, and then, slowly sliding into view, came a
fiery blood-red orb. It lasted so few minutes, this
colour of enchantment. Then it was gone, and she was
seeing only a workaday world, with a blazing sun going
about its business of dispensing its usual molten heat.

She turned a radiant face to her companion; he
laughed across at her, saying, 'Don't forget it is for the
horses that we are out here, not to allow you to indulge
yourself with beautiful sunrises. Come along.'

It is here! It is here! It is here! These three words
flew through Leonie's mind as she also flew—alongside
Ahmed and Shaitan. They were appropriate words,
she felt, having read them at school in an Arabian
poem. And happiness *was* here, this actual moment as
she cantered through an early sun-washed morning.

No more words were exchanged, and at the stables
the same routine was enacted. Her arm wasn't taken
this time as they strolled round to the front of the
house, and, sending a swift sideways glance at him,
Leonie saw those heavy black brows of Ahmed's
meeting in a deep frown which was almost a scowl and
wondered what he was thinking.

Extraneous matters were gone with the wind as they
moved up the narrow stone steps, to be greeted by the
châtelaine of the house, and her brows were like
Ahmed's had been a few seconds ago. 'So you are
back. Did you enjoy your ride?' she asked curtly—and
her tone washed the radiant happiness from Leonie's
face.

She moved a pace forward, but a long arm outstretched barred her passage. Ahmed stood in front of

her, and his voice, still easy and pleasant as it mostly was, held another nuance while saying, 'Yes, we did enjoy our ride—exercising your horses, my dear Mrs Hailstrom. And I quite realise that you are missing being able to ride, but the horses had to be taken out, and I expect Leonie won't be here this evening to do that. We are all going out picnicking today, aren't we?'

'Yes, I expect we are. Don't take any notice of me. You're right—I *do* miss being unable to ride.'

'Yes, but look what's in store for you.' Ahmed was smiling down at her, one of her own malicious smiles, as he continued, 'Something that everyone enjoys—a marvellous sail in a felucca. Now how about that?'

'Yes, how about that?' Mrs Hailstrom returned his smile in kind, then turned as a servant emerged from the house to say breakfast was ready. Ahmed bent down and with a strong arm helped the elderly woman from her chair.

As Leonie prepared to follow her, again a long barricading arm held her back. Drawing her to the side of the archway, that arm shifted and she was pulled in to him. She lay collapsed against the hard-muscled form, feeling her entire body melt into the one holding her, curves and hollows fusing into one entity.

The hand not clasped about her raised her head from where it was resting on the white cashmere sweater. Leonie looked into green eyes only inches away, and wanted only ever to be where she was now. As he saw her expression, Ahmed's breath went in sharply. She felt the rise and fall of his chest against her closely enfolded body.

But he only trailed a long brown finger down her cheek, saying, 'Don't ever let anyone's frown upset you again. There is only one frown you have to take any notice of—and that is mine! No one else, you understand me, Leonie!'

She only nodded as she raised her face further to his and said, 'Do you frown often or get angry, Ahmed? I haven't seen you in that mood yet.'

'Oh, yes, much to my sorrow. I have a temper like Shaitan's sometimes. However, during all my long years I have learnt how to control it. . .mostly, if not always.'

He swung her round to go before him, and traversing the short hallway, they entered a breakfast-room flooded with early morning sunshine. Ahmed seated her in the place she had used last night, then went round to his own seat.

Rashid murmured to him, then answered, 'Yes, my Lord Ahmed.'

Leonie's head swung up. She had noticed the deferential title Fathia had used for him this morning, but had thought that that was only a junior servant's way. Rashid was back now beside their guest, bringing scrambled eggs, toast, and a large cup of tea. Leonie sat drinking her orange juice.

Then it was her turn to have food set before her. Ignoring it, she finished her juice, and sat stirring sugar round and round in her cup. Head bent, eyes downcast, she watched those strong brown fingers buttering toast, lifting scrambled eggs with a fork, then heard their owner saying, 'How is your arm, Mrs Hailstrom? I know broken bones take time to mend.'

'I expect you do know, Ahmed. You get enough broken bones, all of you, in your line of work. But you had better ask Leonie about mine. She was given all the whys and wherefores about it.'

'Now come on, Mrs Hailstrom! You were too if you had condescended to listen.' Leonie turned to the other occupant of the breakfast table, saying, 'She has to go to Cairo in four days or so, then if the X-rays show it's held together properly, which it should have done, seeing she's been so careful. . .'

'Yes, we have been, haven't we?' interrupted an astringent voice from the head of the table. 'I want it better, even if that means doing what those stupid doctors go on about.'

'As I was saying,' continued Leonie placidly, 'she still has to be careful for some weeks. After that she can ride, or drive a car, or whatever. I must also add, Mrs Hailstrom, that with you having Sunna and all the servants you need, I shan't be necessary, so. . .'

'You *will* be necessary. You're coming back here with me for those three weeks. You're my security blanket, Leonie. After that. . .well, after that we'll see!'

Only too pleased to be coming back, Leonie sat silent. It was Ahmed who spoke. 'If it suits you, Mrs Hailstrom, I'll collect you at eleven and take you to meet my guests. And even if it is not a trip to the Middle Oasis, I guarantee to make you comfortable.' A chair was pushed back, a hand raised, and the two women were left alone at the table.

Mrs Hailstrom said, 'That will be all for now, Rashid. We will now just finish our tea.'

The old man bowed and went silently away. His mistress fiddled with table silver for a few moments, then looked up to stare directly at the girl. 'I hope,' she began, 'that you know what you're doing, Leonie. Ahmed is not the sort of man to be played around with.'

Opening her eyes wide, Leonie just gazed silently back.

'And don't come that innocent stuff with me, my

girl! I simply don't know how it happened. . .or how
you ever found time together to meet. I acknowledge
that you didn't behave like lovers; you didn't touch
and hardly spoke, but the rapport, even the tension
between you, was unmistakable.

'About Ahmed's private Arab life I know nothing.
Of his life in Europe one hears some gossip. But
you're here in my house, Leonie, under my protection.
Are you telling me he's seriously interested in you?'

What was she to say? She hated discussing Ahmed.
She asked, 'Would it be so bad if he were?'

'I wouldn't know, Leonie. But it's not a case of boy
meeting girl like in your own country, or even in
England. This is a different land with vastly different
customs. You're a sensible girl, but you'll have to take
care.'

Leonie knew the situation was past the time of
taking care. However, Mrs Hailstrom was standing up,
the subject dismissed, and they went to begin the
morning exercises.

With the morning flying past in a blur one minute,
dragging slowly at others, finally eleven o'clock
arrived. Fathia knocked softly at the door and told
Leonie, 'My lady says she is ready. Will you come?'

'Yes, very well, Fathia. I'll be out directly.' But
Leonie didn't move immediately. She gave another
glance at herself in the mirror. At home in Australia
she would most likely have worn jeans to an affair
such as this. They were more practical for getting into
and out of boats. She glanced over at them, washed
and pressed now as they hung in the wardrobe. But
she was going to meet people who were unknown;
beautiful people, she had been told.

She sighed. She looked again at her reflection, at
the mid-calf length green linen skirt swinging about

her, the sheer voile blouse with its tiny edging of lace
and fine pintucks. She thought it could be worse—but
was it the right thing to wear?

As she had once advised someone else, she hadn't a
wardrobe full of different clothes. So, collecting the
small cream bag she had bought in Cairo, she slung it
over her shoulder by its long thin strap, then went out.

Both she and their conveyance arrived simul-
taneously. Leonie looked at it before glancing at the
man stepping down from the driving seat. It was a
Rover, but not like one she had ever seen before. It
looked a mile long, with huge tyres. Then, as always,
nothing else was registering with her except Ahmed as
he walked across to them.

His manner towards her was distant as it always was
in public. He handed Mrs Hailstrom up into the front
seat and said, 'If you wouldn't mind, Leonie, I'll put
you in the back.'

He came round to swing open the rear door and,
taking her cue from him, she went to step up with only
the barest glance. She found herself caught and held
against him. She heard words in Arabic, then in
English. 'I am a thirty-year-old man who's knocked
around the capitals of Europe as well as of the
East. . .and have sometimes indulged in what has been
offered. But I take one look at you, I come near
enough to touch you, and I find every atom of my self-
control gone. To say what I am saying at this particular
time, in this particular place, is madness, but lord of
heaven, I want you, Leonie!'

Held so close, she looked up at him, frightened a
little by the tension she felt. She said, 'You have only
to ask, Ahmed.'

Then, abruptly, suddenly, that frightening tension
was gone, the form holding her so tightly shaking with

silent laughter. 'That's my girl!' he told her. 'Now, allow me to hand you up.'

Inside, with the big door slammed shut, Leonie glanced round dazedly for a seat, belatedly aware that her entire body was trembling. She collapsed into one immediately behind her. As she sat there, that little scene went round and round in her mind. Nothing between them was clear-cut, and she wondered why. But the roughness of Ahmed's words still echoed, and her body still remembered the grip of those hard forceful arms.

He must have been watching her in the rear-view mirror. He called out as if to prepare her. 'The hotel is coming up. We'll go inside to collect our party.'

'Leonie has to buy a hat, Ahmed,' said a matter-of-fact voice. 'She's too careless in this hot sunshine.'

Aware that Mrs Hailstrom had already had her decided say on that subject this morning, Leonie shrugged, knowing she had been right; she didn't have a suitable hat.

'I'll point the way to the boutique, you'll find plenty of headgear there to choose from,' Ahmed was saying as he helped the older woman down. He came round to do the same service for Leonie, speaking again in his easy pleasant way.

And in the same pleasant way he did direct her. Among what seemed were hundreds of hats, Leonie picked out a green linen one. It would do what it was created for, shade her head and face. She paid for it and, holding it by her side, walked out to the big reception area.

'Oh, here you are,' Ahmed was saying as she joined the group standing in the centre of the foyer.

She said hello politely to the two women—the two beautiful women. She smiled carefully at an elderly, important-looking Egyptian, then laughingly at a handsome polished Greek called George who raised her hand and, instead of kissing the air above it, did the real thing.

'And this is Theo,' was the last person Ahmed was making her known to. Was this another cousin? wondered Leonie. Ahmed had not said so as he had of the others.

A brown finger was raised. Porters in their long coffee-coloured djibbahs began to carry out boxes and hampers to where Hussein was waiting beside the jeep. Most likely our lunch, thought Leonie, as she prepared to follow the exodus. She found the man Theo beside her.

The day, this magic day passed in a haze of wonder and happiness for her. The big vehicle went down the zigzagging path to the river as if moving on smooth asphalt. There, amid laughter and careful help, they all walked the plank into the felucca. There were deckchairs under a canopy up forward for anyone who wanted to use them, and even as they cast off waiters were serving champagne and fruit juice in tall dew-frosted glasses.

Finding her way to the bow of the sailing ship, Leonie settled down to gaze on this wide river or to watch the water chuckling beneath as their passage disturbed it. Ahmed didn't come near her.

However, Theo and Helena did. Leonie liked Helena, thinking her quiet and gentle. She didn't like Theo, and she wished he wouldn't try to claim her attention all the time.

The talk between them was desultory, with apparently all three of them involved in their own thoughts. Leonie did once turn from her absorbed interest in the life of the river going on all about them when Helena asked a question.

'Don't you like Egypt?' she couldn't help enquiring.

'I. . .' The beautiful young girl broke off in mid-sentence, casting a quick glance across to where the older generation were lounging at their ease in the deckchairs; to where Ahmed, with Hussein never far from him, was leaning indolently against the railing, then continued quickly, 'Oh, yes, it is a fascinating country, isn't it?'

'Yes, it is,' answered Leonie, then she returned her gaze to the river. She saw that its banks here were not coloured with vivid greenery as they were further north towards Cairo. Here they gave the impression, as did the land itself, of harshness and aridness.

Then remembering that swiftly broken off sentence, Leonie was sure Helena had been going to say, 'I hate it.'

Did Ahmed know she felt like that? wondered Leonie. Then she decided that she wasn't going to spoil her day by wondering if Ahmed might have a commitment to this girl beside her; that that fact could be the reason why he had never spoken to her outright of his love.

Did he already know that nothing could come of this attraction that bound them together; that it was a star-crossed love destined to flash brilliantly across the firmament for its brief life, then disappear, leaving behind only a memory of what might have been.

Determinedly Leonie thrust these unwanted thoughts away from her. Today was her day; a day out of dreamtime which she was going to enjoy and treasure—and if she had to, if it was all she was going to be allowed, it would always be there to remember.

This day of hot scorching sunshine sailing on a blue river with the man she loved. There, she had said it!

She glanced round to see where he was. But it was not Ahmed coming towards them. It was George, smiling as he held out a hand to Helena, saying, 'I'm sure you don't want to sunbathe. We in our own hot country know differently. Would you care to stroll around and look this funny boat over?'

Placing a hand on her countryman's arm, Helena went gladly, and, gazing with a grin at their departing backs, Leonie felt the look being directed at her from the other occupant of their seat.

'Oh, no!' she muttered. She could do without this. So she asked, smiling impersonally across at him, 'Do you like Egypt, Theo? You'll be going out in the desert soon while I fly home. We're ships that pass in the night and all that sort of thing.'

'Would you come to Athens if I invited you? I. . .we. . .have a large home there,' asked Theo in his strongly accented English.

'Oh, no, I couldn't do that! I'm a working girl. I'm not here socially, you know. I will be leaving for home almost immediately,' she told him, adding to herself, There, that should do it!

Before any reply could reach her a shadow fell across them. Hussein was bowing deferentially before her. 'Lady,' he said, 'the Lord Ahmed says will you come for drinks?'

Thankfully she rose. She said over a shoulder, 'You should go for a drink too, Theo,' and walked forward as Hussein stood aside to allow her passage. She subsided into the chair being pulled out for her, Ahmed dropping into the one beside it. He wasn't showing any favours, however; he had Helena on his other side.

She accepted the tall cold glass offered to her, unaware of what she was actually doing. Ahmed was so close, she felt the brush of his thigh as he turned laughing to answer a question.

Sipping her drink, which she found was just fruit juice, she gazed under downcast lashes at the long legs so near her own as they lay outspread in cream linen slacks. She felt the smooth silk covering his arm as he leaned back in his chair again.

She gazed ahead out at the river, seeing, yet not aware of, the white sails skimming about them; the small boats and barges going about their business of a working day; the silken waters reflecting the deep, incredibly blue turquoise sky.

The felucca turned, the liquid in her loosely held glass slopping against its rim. A strong brown hand had suddenly enclosed her own, tightening both holds. The fruit juice settled down, as the felucca sailed serenely back the way it had come.

Ahmed's hand dropped. Following its passage with her eyes, Leonie saw it fall between the chairs, and clench. She knew then absolutely that what he had said this morning behind the Land Rover was true. He *did* want her; but would anything ever come of this love? she wondered, trying to fight desolation away.

Finishing her drink, she handed back the glass to a waiter, refusing another, and saw just a short distance away the islands they were going to visit.

CHAPTER EIGHT

WAVING to her employer, who said irascibly that she had no intention of traipsing up there to see a tomb of someone she had known when alive, Leonie moved up the rocky landscape behind Ahmed and Mrs Paulus. She noted that, just as he behaved to her in public, he didn't lend a helping hand to the older lady either. Theo was attempting to do that very thing for her, but she stepped back to walk beside Helena.

She didn't go far inside the Mausoleum; she didn't like it. So she edged out among other tourists who were being escorted around. Outside, she gazed down at their felucca riding tranquilly on the placid, glistening water, and drew a deep, satisfied breath. She also knew even before he spoke who had come so quietly along to stand beside her.

'Not interested in tombs, Leonie? I expected, knowing your predilection for history, that you would be.'

'Oh, indeed I am! In pyramids, and in the times of the Pharaohs, because one wonders what they were really like; what they thought of their life here in this world—five thousand years ago—and why they did the things they did. But the Aga Khan comes from a modern world, and he was a Persian prince. Why here? Why not a tomb in his own land?'

'Because he was the head of the Ismaili Muslims, a very large community in Egypt.'

They had been strolling companionably down the path when they were caught up in a flurry of movement as the others came along to surround them. Leonie listened, smiling at some of the caustic remarks being uttered; but suddenly she wasn't smiling or thinking of acid comments. One of the large stones with which the path was amply supplied twisted under her sandal, and she was falling. Ahmed, fingers iron-hard, reached out from nowhere. She was caught and brought upright. The hand fell away.

Mrs Hailstrom, ensconced comfortably in her chair beside the important-looking Egyptian Ibrahaim Pasha—who must have been included despite Ahmed's having said he would be the only non-European present—asked them maliciously, 'Have you all decided what you are going to do about your own tombs?'

'I don't know how you can suggest anything so outlandish, Grace! As if people like us ever think of that sort of thing! Now, I'm going to wash my hands before lunch, which is, Ahmed has told me, in twenty minutes.' Mrs Paulus sounded as if she was not amused.

So her employer's Christian name was Grace, thought Leonie, also thinking that she didn't sound or behave like a Grace. But she went smilingly with her as they followed Helena's mother inside to wash.

Returning to the deck minutes later, she saw that they were approaching another jetty. But this one was set in a vastly different landscape. And, enchanted, Leonie strolled through what was beauty growing in such vivid profusion, Theo on one side of her, Ibrahaim Pasha on the other.

She turned to the Egyptian, saying, 'They're wonderful, these gardens, aren't they? At least here is one Englishman who has left something lasting and beautiful behind.'

'Oh, don't run away with the idea that we Egyptians

dislike the British. We don't! We are happy, however, to be running our own country. Did you know that the young Sheikh Ahmed's father——' he pointed to where their host was strolling between the two older women '—was an officer in the British Army during the war?'

'No, I didn't! I wouldn't have dreamed of such a thing! I was under the impression that the Wallifa were desert Arabs,' ejaculated Leonie, turning this new information over in her mind.

But her attention came back to the present as she heared Ahmed's voice saying, 'Along here.'

'Along here' meant passing a sign which said 'No Admittance'. She saw Ahmed smile and raise an eyebrow at one of her companions, and it was not Theo. 'We can't have our lunch spoilt by tourists wandering about, now can we? So. . . I might be able to do some favours. I expect some in return!'

'And get them, apparently,' was the dry answer from Ibrahaim Pasha.

'Oh, yes, certainly.' Ahmed was laughing as he saw them all through, then replaced the No Admittance sign.

They emerged into a clearing where folding tables held food and drink. Also, the four canvas chairs from the felucca were again in evidence; how they had been transported was a mystery. Nothing had been seen either of them or their porters and waiters. There were also fat cushions and rugs.

Escorting his two companions towards the chairs, their host told them, 'The other two are for anyone who wants them; the cushions are also for anyone who wants them.' A black eyebrow went up again, a smile went the rounds of them all.

One of the two extra seats was taken. Ibrahaim

Pasha sank into it and said with decision, 'Now, young Sheikh Ahmed, as it happened in the old days, ply me with sensuous food and drink; the other ingredients are already here—lovely young houris from paradise,' he bowed to the two girls, 'conversation from intelligent women,' he bowed again to the two older ladies, 'and more importantly. . . I hope. . .information!' Here, his little bow was directed completely towards Ahmed.

Ahmed only laughed, both his hands going out in a throwaway gesture. 'Be my guest,' he answered, 'in all things.'

Helena's elbow was caught and she was guided to one of the cushions by George. Again she went willingly.

Leonie's elbow was also taken hold of and Theo said, 'Come along, Leonie. We'll take these two cushions.'

What else could she do? Go, or try to pull away from that tight hold? Well, she could go, but with a determined sharp tug she pulled her arm free, saying, 'Yes, of course I'll come, but don't be silly, Theo. You don't have to guide me that little way.'

Theo was quite content for this to happen, having got what he wanted. He began to talk to her about Athens as waiters started to circulate. He wasn't left in sole possession of her attention for long, however. Ahmed had collected another cushion, and setting it under a date palm soaring to the blue heavens high above them, sat down to lean against it. And again, as earlier on in the felucca, Leonie felt the big body's movement as he went about his business of directing the servants.

Being offered a tray which had of course been presented to Ahmed first, she took one of the long fluted glasses. Fingers clasping the coolness of it, she sipped, then turned to glance at her companion. She found her gaze meeting a wide glittering smile as he raised his own glass to salute her. 'Enjoy this day which has been given to you, Leonie,' he said, and upending his glass drank deeply from it. It held champagne.

Then he had turned his attention from her to his other guests. But what did she care? Ahmed was drinking champagne. . .alcohol! She drank her own glass right down, but, taking another being offered in exchange for her empty one, she set it down carefully on the rug beside her. She wasn't used to wine in the middle of the day, and she wanted to keep her mind clear to do expressly what Ahmed had told her to do—enjoy the day.

She ate the food offered to her; she drank fruit juice when it also made its appearance. She allowed the beauty of the exquisite gardens to flow into her being. She also listened absently to Theo, murmuring an occasional yes or no. She was aware only of the lounging, lithe body so close to her.

The long, leisurely meal finished, they strolled back, taking their time. The felucca, looking very familiar by now, was waiting for them to re-embark. They didn't sail up and down the river this time, but made for the further bank immediately. Leonie wondered where the time had gone. The sun was still in the heavens, but sinking towards the west more clearly every minute.

Driving to the hotel, Leonie heard their host say to his guests, 'I'll be with you for dinner, and with you too, Ibrahaim Pasha, if you will so honour me.'

She didn't hear the reply; Theo was talking up at her. But then their driver had slid behind the wheel, and the big vehicle was moving off in a scatter of gravel, leaving behind their erstwhile companions grouped before the façade of the large, imposing building.

Ahmed escorted Mrs Hailstrom up their own short steps and on to the veranda, throwing one word over his shoulder at her. 'Wait!'

So she waited the short minute before he was back. He swung the large rear door of the Land Rover further open so that their two figures were sheltered from other eyes.

'Did you enjoy your day, Leonie?' he asked, and a long brown finger stroked down her cheek.

Gazing up at him, she only nodded, then replied as a black eyebrow went high, 'Yes, of course I did.'

'Well, an early night won't go amiss, as you went riding to meet the sun this morning. Lucky you! *I* have to do my duty to my father's guests, which, thank God or Allah, will be finished in the next couple of days. My father is back—at least, he is in Cairo, I have been informed. Now, I will be busy all day tomorrow, both with my Aunt Helen, and business. However, for being a good girl always, would you like to see the desert by moonlight?'

Flustered by this abrupt change of subject, knowing it had been moonlight for some nights, although she hadn't seen much of it, Leonie answered, 'Of course I would, but around here isn't classed as desert, is it?'

'No, it is not. But if you don't mind a late start I can take you riding and you can see the moon come up over the desert.'

'Oh, Ahmed!' There was no need for an answer of yes or no; acceptance was there in every tone of her voice.

Ahmed took hold of both her hands and, raising

them, didn't bestow his caress in the European fashion, but turned them and, lowering his dark head, pressed lips upon each of the blue-veined wrists in turn. It was not a fleeting kiss either, and as those scorching caresses still continued, sending her every pulse jumping, Leonie sent her whole body collapsing into his.

She found herself stood away, and, opening eyes which had been fast closed, she saw a face almost strange to her, with white indentations shadowing those sculptured lips and deep stark creases between those black brows. And when he spoke his tone was neither easy or pleasant.

'I'll have to stop this,' he said. 'I can only take so much.'

A hand reached out, indicating that she go before him, then the big back door of the Rover was slammed shut. That still strange voice said, 'I'll call for you at nine-thirty tomorrow night, Leonie,' and without escorting her to either the steps or the veranda, Ahmed had slipped under the wheel. The cobbled path rattled as a foot went down hard on an accelerator.

Leonie walked slowly inside and knocked on her employer's door. She said softly as they did the exercises, 'You're doing very well, you know.'

'Yes, I am, aren't I?' came the complacent reply. 'And did I tell you that we're going to Cairo the day after tomorrow to have those damned X-rays? Then a few short weeks will see the finish of it and I can ride again. We'll only be staying the one day, then come home on the following morning's plane.'

'If that's what you want to do, Mrs Hailstrom. You know I'll be happy to stay.' Here, Leonie looked directly at the elderly woman, and allowed a gamine grin to illuminate her face as she continued, 'As someone else I know once said, I'll take whatever God or Allah provides.'

So the next night, sitting waiting on the parapet where only two nights ago she had been with Ahmed, Leonie glanced out at the dark night; no, she thought, it wasn't really dark. Starshine gave to the atmosphere a glimmering luminosity. Light from stars that were strange to her, she thought, glancing up at them.

Still, even if she could see the face of her watch, it was no use looking at it. The last time she had done so, it had been only nine-fifteen. If Ahmed had told her nine-thirty, then that was when he would arrive. So she sat quietly, allowing the night to flow about her, having decided not to wonder what was going to happen between them; to let whatever eventuated take its course.

Hearing low voices from outside their fenced gardens, she took no notice. Few cars passed this way, but Egyptians on foot and horses did. She almost jumped when a knock came on her door, but went quickly to open it. Karim said, 'The Lord Ahmed is here.'

Catching up a cardigan, Leonie followed him along the hallway through a silent house. Mrs Hailstrom and Gertrude Ferguson were out at their weekly bridge party.

Ahmed had not come round to her verandaed room. He had come formally to the front door. He stood there in his riding gear and looking at her gravely, said, 'Good evening, Leonie.'

All she replied was, 'Hello.'

He was adding, however, taking the cardigan from her, 'You won't need this,' and handing it to a waiting Karim. So, without it, she walked beside him down

the steps and out along the front driveway to join a
small group of men and horses quietly waiting.

One of the men was standing as usual beside
Shaitan's stirrup. But Ahmed turned to the horse
beside the black stallion, saying as he took a garment
from off its saddle, 'This mare is one of ours, Leonie.
You will find she is very easy to ride. Come here for a
moment, though.'

She went to him, and found he was throwing a cloak
round her shoulders, then fastening it across her breast
with a large clasp. 'You will find you will need this
when we get further out,' he told her, then held a
stirrup for her to step into.

The reins in her hands, getting the feel of the mount
beneath her, she found herself riding beside Ahmed.
Ali was out in front, with Mustafa and Hussein riding
guard behind. Leonie pulled the enveloping cloak
about her even if she didn't need it yet. It smelt of
Ahmed! Then she admonished herself for thinking
such a thing. The aroma it gave off was one of
sandalwood. And always she knew whenever the
fragrance of sandalwood was present, it would bring
back to her the memory of Ahmed.

So now she rode, silently for the most part, towards
the cluster of lights which outlined the big hotels, and
further ones of the Arab village. Then abruptly, without any sign of them being directed, their horses
swerved and they were riding directly westwards.

Her face raised to the breeze that *was* getting colder,
Leonie allowed her thoughts to roam. To home in
Australia, where she had often ridden at night-time,
some of it spent in working cattle. But she knew,
without consciously thinking about it, that the atmosphere of this land about her was so vastly different.
She swung a swift glance at her companion. His profile

was all she could discern. It showed only that austere sternness it always carried when in repose.

Then she smiled to herself, suddenly incredibly happy inside. She had seen it when it hadn't been in repose!

They cantered on, once being passed by other riders, who, without greetings, dropped over to allow their passage. And once a helicopter with its engines shaking the air-waves about them passed across the heavens. Ahmed was looking up at it, she saw, and she wondered where it came from.

Then, abruptly, there were no more signs of civilisation. They could have been in an empty world, when unexpectedly she felt the ground beneath her mount's hooves change. They were riding on sand.

They rode on for another half-hour or so when, once again, without seeming directions, the entire group had come to a halt. Dismounting, walking across to her, Ahmed said, 'Journey's end, Leonie. Down you come.' She saw that the horses were being led away, and that her companion was hollowing out a seat within one of the dunes rising about them. He spread the big cloak that he too had been riding in and taking her hand, led her to it, saying, 'Well, here it is Leonie! The desert! We'll see what the moon does to it.'

As she sank down, the man dropped also, placing an arm behind her to bring her to him. But it was an impersonal clasp. He said, 'We have ten minutes before the moon rises. Tell me about yourself, Leonie.'

She turned to him in that close proximity, but only replied, sounding puzzled, 'What do you mean? There's nothing to tell you. I'm just an ordinary girl.'

'Oh, no, for the life of me I wouldn't call you just

ordinary. But I *would* like to know where you come from; what relations you have. . .' Ahmed's words stopped.

'I'm from Australia, as you know, and I haven't any relatives. Well, maybe some cousins, but I don't know them.'

Leonie paused for a moment, sad as always when thinking of her parents. Beside her Ahmed moved restlessly, so she resumed. 'My father was lucky in winning a land ballot, because the land was all he ever wanted. All he ever loved—except for my mother. And as I was an only child, my father treated me as the boy he would have liked; putting me up in front of his saddle before I could ride, and on a little mare from my second birthday. Riding is second nature to me. I could even ride Shaitan,' she was saying pensively.

'No, you bloody well could not!' These words, coming in a so emphatic tone, brought Leonie's lounging figure instinctively upright.

'I've never heard you swear before, Ahmed, or even heard you speak in that manner,' she told him unhappily.

'Oh, you *have* heard me swear before, but in Arabic, which you wouldn't understand. But now, I'm telling you, I never want to see you near Shaitan. Understand me, Leonie! Even Hussein, when I'm away, exercises him on a long rein. He never rides him. I'm the only one Shaitan will allow to do that.'

'I only meant that I *can* ride. . .very well. Even buck-jumpers, which is what we call untamed horses in Australia. I helped to break in our own. We were quite poor, you know, Ahmed, and couldn't afford the price for sale horses.'

'I'd like to swear again in English,' said Ahmed

harshly. 'What kind of a life was that for a girl like you?'

Leonie bent over, gurgling with laughter at that outraged tone. 'Don't be silly, Ahmed,' she told him. 'I had a very happy life. I had love and care always around me—even if I did have to work hard on the property and at my school work. The only unhappy time in my life was when my father died and we had to sell up and go to Brisbane. It was there that I finished school and got my present job. Now, it's your turn. I only know about you from bits of gossip I've picked up. I know you belong to a powerful Arab tribe and that Mrs Hailstrom says you're wealthy. I know you have relations. . .and I've wondered all the time, remembering your behaviour to me, if you're married?'

Oh, dear, she *had* said those words. She *had* wondered! But she certainly had not meant to speak of it—especially not tonight. Tonight was to be like that magic day of yesterday—a slice garnered out of time. What in the name of heaven had made those words come out?

She felt the arm around her tighten; she also felt the ripples that flowed through his body, ripples that she had come to associate with that silent laughter of his. She turned angrily, as if to move away, but the arm around her only tightened.

'You know, Leonie,' said a voice still holding an edge of laughter within it, 'I didn't realise that you would think that. Mrs Hailstrom, I expect, might do so, knowing our customs. . .and my age. But we, you and I, have been together, have spoken together quite intimately more than once. And I've shown you, haven't I, how I feel about you? That you could think what you apparently have done just didn't occur to me.

'No, I am not married, but there are other considerations that need. . .Oh, look!'

Leonie didn't want to look; she wanted to hear about those other considerations. But, held so firmly close, she saw Ahmed's profile turned from her, that so austere profile. So she looked to where he was pointing.

Straight in front of her concentrating gaze appeared the faintest line of luminescence, whether on the horizon or on the far stretch of the desert before her, she couldn't tell. But then it was spreading, not in silver, but in orange. Within minutes, however, within seconds almost, a sliver of round silver showed, and as she watched the moon rose against her vision. A vast full orb turning from orange to silver, suddenly sailing free and shedding its brilliant light across a desert not only coated in silver, but in deep dark ebony.

Leonie drew a deep unsteady breath and reached out a hand to where she knew a long brown one might be. She felt it taken, and Ahmed spread wide her fingers, entwining them between his own. He rested them both on an outstretched thigh as they sat, silent, just gazing before them. Ahmed at what was his birthright, Leonie at the magic of it. She sighed.

And abruptly, Ahmed had turned, and with her body still enfolded within his arm had lifted her back on the cloak-covered sand. Leaning over her, his face showed unsmiling in the brightness of the moonlight. Then with fingers that revealed no haste, he sprang open the big clasp fastening her big cloak, slipping his arm between it and her body. He did speak. . .but in Arabic.

Then his lips were upon hers, moving slowly back

and forth as if searching for a remembered sensation. Without volition Leonie sent her free arm to clasp tightly about his neck, deliberately merging her entire form into the one stretched above and beside her. She felt warm fingers undo the top buttons of her shirt; she felt them do as his lips were doing, move back and forth above a lace-edged cleavage. She shivered.

But his lips had stopped their sensuous exploration of her own, and had begun to travel; down along a thrown-back exposed throat to pause for a brief second as they covered a jumping pulse. Then once again those slow kisses had resumed their journey until the were moving back and forth along the path his fingers had already broken. In a far distant world, she wasn't aware of the shudder which convulsed her whole system.

But it was in that far distant world that she became aware of the coiling ecstasy mounting within her as those scorching caresses branded the smooth, bare skin with his own possession. Without conscious volition she went into him, fusing her own soft curves into hard-muscled hollows. They lay as one entity, while up above a cold, impersonal moon looked down.

Low in his throat, Leonie heard the man above her speak, but words passed over emotions that took in no outside events; that were aware only of body fusing to body, of senses that were floating as desire and passion imposed their own command. She didn't even hear her own voice saying, 'Ahmed. . . Ahmed. . .'

But that hard-muscled body had suddenly, unexpectedly twisted, turning aside from her. His voice, husky and strained, spoke in Arabic, then changed to English. 'I *did* intend to make love to you out here in the desert. . .just a little. I wanted to. . .but I should have known better.' Here a low ironic laugh erupted, and he said, 'Leonie, I'm sorry.'

For a moment only silence reigned, then he was continuing, 'I have explanations to make and so many things to see to before I. . .' He turned to help her upright, but violently, sharply she pushed the hands aside. Aware that her bones were still melted jelly, she allowed anger to help her scramble up unaided— deep, throbbing anger.

Remembering how she had acted, how she had given reciprocation to his every caress, and what she had offered him, she felt nausea well deep inside at this unlooked-for repulse. What was the matter with him? Or most likely the fault lay with her, she thought wildly. He *had* shown he wanted her, oh, yes, he had, she knew, remembering. But apparently he had not wanted her enough to overcome this barrier which seemed to be between them. And just look how she had behaved! Sick, actually nauseated, all she wanted now was to get away—both from him, and from this place, this Egypt.

'Please take me home,' her cold voice asked him. 'I can't say I'll get a bus or a taxi. But I want to get away. I never want to see you ever again, Ahmed Wallifa!'

He moved two steps towards her, but, stepping back quickly, ungainly in the shifting sand, she said again, 'I only want to go home!'

'Very well. Button your shirt before we do, though.' Ahmed's breath had quickened, the sound harsh in the quiet night about them, but his voice had returned to its normal pleasant tone. He wouldn't be able to see the burning, ashamed flush of colour that stained her cheeks, the whole of her face and neck, as his words reached her.

And it was unsteadily that she raised trembling fingers to fumble with buttons and buttonholes.

Again Ahmed moved a step forward as if to help, but angrily she motioned him away. 'I'll manage,' she said acidly. 'I realise you wouldn't want your men to see your companion dishevelled and untidy!'

'No, I would not! And that is not for my sake!'

'Of course it isn't. Hussein has already informed me of that fact, the morning when I was on your boat. He said his Lord could do anything. . .that it was for me all the trouble was being taken. Well, understand me, Sheikh of the Wallifa, there will be no more need to take trouble about me. I'm going home!'

'Fasten that clasp,' was all he said, and this time his tone was neither easy or pleasant. It was harsh and grating.

Unable to close the unfamiliar fastening, Leonie saw Ahmed stretch out a hand to do so, and again she moved back. But that hand, hard and callused from working with horses, gripped her shoulder, and this time it was his anger that showed. He didn't speak, however, he just snapped shut the clasp, then sent a peculiar call echoing over the desert. Then, with his behaviour to her as it always was when they were not alone, he indicated that she go before him.

CHAPTER NINE

LEONIE sat in a chair drawn up to the door leading out to her veranda, once again watching the horizon lighten as dawn was about to break. She sat there, listless, the strain of deathly tiredness showing. There was no way she was going out there, where she had once sat so happily with Ahmed when he had come to make arrangements with her. . . Arrangements! How many affairs could that word extend to!

Behind her was the bed on which she had tried so desperately to sleep and had found that even dozing was beyond her. Well, she felt a little better now. Her decision made, the journey home finally endured, she had decided that with a different land, a different environment around her, she could put this place and its inhabitants behind her.

As the horizon before her began to show the vivid colours of sunrise, Leonie rose from her chair, turning abruptly away. She didn't want to see it! She closed and locked the big suitcase and stood it beside the door; she checked the room and her overnight case once again, then leaving it and her large shoulder-bag on the bed, opened her door and walked along the tiled elegance of the hallway into the breakfast-room.

Here was no table set for the meal. Of course it wasn't; it was too early. But, never having summoned a servant before, she knew of only one way. So, taking a deep breath, she raised the small hammer and struck the brass gong as Mrs Hailstrom did when wanting Rashid or Karim.

She walked to the door and waited. She didn't care about summoning one of the men; she didn't care about anything at all except getting home. And one of their compatriots had been the cause of this stark pain behind her eyes. She had taken two aspirins; tea now would probably clear it up before she went in to Mrs Hailstrom. It was some minutes before Rashid came. Of course it would be him. Karim had been waiting up for her return some time during the small hours of this morning.

She had slipped from her mount, ignoring the hand Ahmed raised to help her. However, for the benefit of the other three Arabs, she had said, her voice once more her own after that more than an hour's ride back, 'Thank you for taking me to see the moon rise. Goodnight!'

But she could have been addressing empty air, Ahmed was still behind her as she mounted the steps. Karim came from the hallway to greet her, and turning to gesture her before him, saw Ahmed. He swung back.

Leonie didn't care, she didn't even smile ironically at this fact of Arab behaviour. She also didn't hear the curt order—certainly not a request—her erstwhile companion gave to Karim. By then she was in her own room, the door fast shut.

But for now, here was Rashid hurrying. He stopped short on seeing that it was Leonie and not his mistress who had rung, giving a swift glance around. She smiled as pleasantly as she could manage at him, saying, 'I know it's early, Rashid, but I have a headache, so do you think you could make me some tea? Nothing to eat, just tea.'

'Of course, lady. I'll bring it immediately.' Rashid bowed slightly and turned. Leonie moved out on to the veranda and sat with her back to the newborn day. It was a little more than the immediately that Rashid had stated when the old man arrived with the silver tea-tray.

Drinking the hot, strong liquid, Leonie finished the first cup, then poured another. Lying back in her chair, she sipped slowly, watching the hands of her watch slip past, and at seven-thirty she rose to make her way unhappily along two hallways to her employer's suite of rooms.

She knocked and waited. Sunna opened the door. 'Could I see you for a moment, please, Mrs Hailstrom?' began Leonie, as she walked across the cool mosaic tiles. She found herself interrupted

'You're up and dressed early, Leonie. Good, because I wanted to see you before breakfast. I gave you a cheque in Cairo for the first three weeks of your stay here, so this one is for the next three. You can bank or change it in Cairo today.'

Making no move to take the slip of white paper held out to her, Leonie stood straighter and said, stammering a little—this opening was not what she had planned, 'I. . . I can't take it, Mrs Hailstrom. I know I. . . I said I'd be happy to remain here. . .but I've thought that as your arm is almost better—which I imagine the X-rays will prove today—I'd be only taking your money under false pretences. Having Sunna always with you, you actually don't need me any more. . .'

'Really, Leonie!' came the interruption. 'Good as Sunna is, and I hope I'll never be without her, she doesn't have your training and know-how. I told you, you're my security blanket and I need you for the whole six weeks the doctor spoke of. So now here, take your cheque. Anyhow, Sunna can't come with me to Cairo today, so I *am* depending on you.'

As the girl standing so straight and rigid before her made no effort to do so, the older woman turned round and through the looking-glass kept her eyes on Leonie. 'Of course,' she went on, 'if you haven't been happy here, if you find this place too far from civilisation and you're disliking it very much, I quite understand. I'll ask Mr Hamid to either fix you up with some tours if you'd like that, or your flight home. I'm sorry, of course, but there it is. . . I realise it's not very entertaining for a young girl up here, so. . .' Mrs Hailstrom picked up a comb and began to run it through her hair.

Miserably, Leonie just stood there. This woman had been so good to her. She had been treated more as a daughter or a guest than a paid employee.

She made herself say, 'You must know very well that I've liked being up here; that I've loved every minute of my stay. It's just. . .it's just I don't feel I'm needed. And I *would* rather go. . .'

'Well, if you like it here, if you aren't bored. . .and I need you, which I do, you can surely stay for the extra three weeks?'

What was she to say? wondered Leonie. She hadn't imagined her employer would react as she was doing. Mrs Hailstrom was a proud woman and it was not like her to ask for help or favours. So she herself would just have to keep out of Ahmed's way, and return here for the next three weeks. She drew a ragged breath, saying, 'If you want me, Mrs Hailstrom, then of course I'll stay.' Glancing at the woman watching her in the mirror, she gave a half-smile, and turned, moving towards the door.

She didn't see the smile of satisfaction that was

being sent after her reflected back, or hear the muttered, 'I handled that better than you could ever do, Ahmed. But then I'm not so involved!'

And back in her own room, Leonie looked down at the packed cases, then hauled the large one on to a chair. Unlocking it, she quickly began to hang away dresses and skirts, slacks and blouses; to pile underclothing and incidentals into drawers. Seeing their untidiness, she knew Fathia would only straighten them without thinking, without even mentioning the state of her room.

But if she left a suitcase packed ready to leave, that would be a different matter. Because servants did talk, and Hussein and Mustafa did fraternise with Mohammed, who would no doubt talk with Rashid. . . Finishing, she was just putting the case into a far corner of the built-in wardrobe when a knock came upon her door.

'Breakfast is waiting, lady,' called Fathia.

'Very well, I'll be out directly, Fathia,' Leonie answered, then, taking a comb out of her bag, combed her hair straight and patted a tissue over a face grown hot with exertion. There! she told herself. Now I look calm and collected. And I'll go to Cairo calm and collected—and come back and behave the same way. But then I *am* going home. I don't want to be with Ahmed again. I just don't understand him. . .or the way he behaves. Perhaps Kipling was right saying that never the twain shall meet—or if they do, it doesn't seem to work.

So, joining her employer in the small sun-room, Leonie accepted the orange juice Rashid poured for her, but waved away his queries about food.

'Oh, I forgot to ask you, Leonie. Did you enjoy

your desert by moonlight? I hope you did, because I
didn't enjoy my bridge.'

'Yes, I did! It sounds corny, I know, to talk about
seeing the desert by moonlight. But it's such a fantastic
scene there's no wonder people do talk about it.
However, I'm sorry about your bridge game.' To
herself, her tone sounded as it usually did, giving
nothing away, thought Leonie thankfully.

'Yes, I think it is too. I still remember my first
experience of seeing the moon rise over it, but of
course I was with my beloved Giles at the time.
Actually, I expect, it all comes down to what one is
interested in. . . Yes, all right,' she answered Karim,
who came in to tell her that the car was outside.

So, collecting her shoulder-bag and overnight case,
Leonie made her way outside. Climbing the two high
steps of the Land Rover, she felt her tummy muscles
flip unsteadily. Would everything, she asked herself
acidly, remind her of the things she had done with
Ahmed? Well, things at home wouldn't!

She walked beside Mrs Hailstrom, who was being
accompanied by Karim carrying her suitcase, which
Leonie took from him as they walked up the steps of
the small plane.

Again the memory of Ahmed intruded when they
took their seats. But Leonie leaned back and closed
her eyes, determinedly making herself think only of
home. Arriving at Cairo, she walked cautiously
through this crowded and exotic place that she
remembered.

Although acknowledging that there was no way
Ahmed could be here, that he was taking guests out to
his father's home at the Middle Oasis, she yet kept her
gaze resolutely away from any white-clad Arabs that
passed her by. She wanted no reminders of what he

looked like. There were more than enough memories that jumped out at her from ordinary things.

The same big black limousine which they had used the last time they were here was waiting. Shepheards Hotel was also waiting, familiar to her as they entered and walked across the vast marble floor.

'We've just time for a quick wash and lunch, instead of doing some shopping, Leonie,' said Mrs Hailstrom. 'Then after that damn X-ray, and the doctor, we'll see what time we have left.'

But it was after four o'clock when they were finally departing from the doctor's surgery, happy at being given good reports from both places. But her employer's smile was shortlived as she was accosted by a figure waiting for her outside the clinic.

It was an Arab in the familiar clothes of the Wallifa. Standing aside quietly waiting, listening to the rapid crossfire in Arabic, Leonie then followed the older woman downstairs and out to the waiting vehicle.

There came a curt command to the driver, and as she settled back, Mrs Hailstrom's face had lost that satisfied look it had worn when she had heard those results. 'That was one of Sheikh Hassan's young men,' she told Leonie. 'He's sent word for us to go straight back to the hotel and stay there. There seems to be some unrest in the city and we're not to go out. He'll be there to escort us to the plane in the morning.'

'Good heavens, Mrs Hailstrom, what can he mean by unrest? The streets are crowded as they usually are. Everything looks normal.'

'Well, normal or not, no one ignores a warning from the Wallifa. Yusef has flown home to the Middle Oasis, Ahmed isn't here, and Hassan also leaves in the early morning after we depart. Here we are.' Descending as nimbly from the big vehicle as she could manage while still protecting her arm, Mrs Hailstrom gave a rapid order to their driver, then walked straight-backed into the hotel.

Making for the lifts, she eyed a group of tourists sitting round waiting, suitcases stacked about them, then turned abruptly to make for the reception desk. Expecting her to begin questioning, Leonie glanced at her face and away again, surprised at seeing only the usual smiling countenance as she dealt with Mr Hamid.

Again keeping her glance turned away, Leonie heard with incredulity the older woman asking if it would be possible to book for dinner at one of the nightclubs; not the El Sahara, she said, that was for tourists, but one of the more select ones. Leonie remembered that the El Sahara was the one to which Greg had taken her and. . . She forced her thoughts away from what had happened afterwards.

'Certainly, Mrs Hailstrom,' she was answered. 'It will be no trouble to get you a reservation to wherever you would like to go.'

'Very well. I'll think it over and ring down to you. I could even change my mind and dine here. It all depends on my arm.'

Leonie stopped herself in time from shaking her head. Mrs Hailstrom was the limit! Whatever would she do when she had no sore arm for an excuse whenever she wanted one? Leonie wondered. And she wondered more as they moved over to the lift. Away from the reception area and Mr Hamid, a deep frown had come to rest between her employer's eyes. However, she remained silent until they had reached her own room. There she stood quietly, deep in thought.

Unable to prevent herself, Leonie exclaimed, 'You're not thinking of going out, are you? Even if Sheikh Hassan is wrong in his warning, a busy crowded nightclub is still to be avoided for the next three weeks.'

The words brought Mrs Hailstrom out of her trance. 'Don't be silly, Leonie,' she said curtly. 'Of course I'm not. I just wanted to see if Hamid knows anything. He apparently doesn't.'

'Would Sheikh Hassan know? You said his man only mentioned unrest. It could be just a silly rumour flying around—they do, you know.'

'If you think, Leonie, that he went to all the trouble of searching for me, just to tell me of a rumour, you don't know Hassan. . .or the Wallifa. They have ears everywhere; they trade across every country of the Middle East.

'It was getting in touch with Ahmed about some special racing camels that his men are delivering that brought all this about. Of course Hassan mentioned this. . .rumour, as you call it, and Ahmed asked him to keep an eye on us. It was, of course, you that Ahmed would be worried about. . .only, I expect, that we might be caught up in some demonstrating mob. There are rather more volatile people here than in Australia, you know,' said her companion drily.

'How silly!' interrupted Leonie. 'There's nothing between Ahmed and myself any longer. I was going home this morning until I spoke with you. If there's anyone they want to protect, it would most likely be you.'

'No, it would not. You might think there's nothing more between you two, Leonie, but I don't! Neither does Ahmed. He told me you'd had some sort of a disagreement, and that you might. . .just might possibly say you wanted to leave. He apparently doesn't intend that to happen. So, to please him, I told you this morning that I needed you.'

CHAPTER TEN

'I DON'T believe it, Mrs Hailstrom!' Leonie was too astounded and mortified to think of how she sounded. She went on, 'How could he have asked you that? You wouldn't have seen him after I was with him in the desert.'

'Oh, but I did see him, my dear child. Last night! He had Sunna come and wake me. Look here, Leonie, I don't know what your. . .your disagreement was about. However, I don't for the least second think Ahmed has tried to seduce you. . .'

'And wouldn't you be right!' interjected Leonie so softly that her employer didn't hear it, but was continuing,

'He had taken you from my house, and. . .and he's the most straitlaced man I know. And believe me, that's something to say about a man who's half Arab and half Greek. Because men of both those countries are not noted for such an attitude concerning their emotional affairs—except of course where their own women are concerned.'

Hearing Mrs Hailstrom's words, turning them over in her mind, Leonie felt that iron band of depression still enfold her. She said slowly, carefully, 'But, Mrs Hailstrom, I don't know how to take him. He does act at times as if. . .he finds me attractive. But then he closes up and turns away. I did wonder if he was married, but he told me no. Still, there must be something in his life to make him behave the way he does.'

'If Ahmed told you he's not married, then he's not! I *would* have thought, knowing his age, and their customs, that he could have been. No one would have known, or have had to know, except his own people. Still, he possibly has his own reasons for whatever he's doing. You'll just have to wait and see.

'Now, I think I'll ring through and order the most exotic dinner the hotel kitchens can provide. We'll have them send it down and set it out on a table, complete with a bottle of their most expensive champagne!'

'What's wrong with the dining-room upstairs itself?' asked Leonie, laughing.

'Nothing! And also I think it would be wise for you to share this room tonight. So off you go now and change if you want to, and bring back your night things with you when you come back.'

Beginning to reply with some amusement, Leonie looked at the serious face opposite, then said instead, 'OK, I'm on my way.' And in her own room she changed swiftly into a loose green linen dress she took out of her case, before returning to discover what the kitchen had provided in the way of an exotic meal.

Afterwards, because of what happened later, Leonie never remembered much about that dinner. She enjoyed what she ate of it. She had a glass of champagne. Then she sat idly listening to Mrs Hailstrom as she wondered aloud what all the rumours had been about.

The waiters arrived to clear away and set the furniture back to rights, then bowed themselves away. Leonie turned down both beds, switched on the bedlamps, then, setting Mrs Hailstrom to do the exercises still required, told her she was slipping next door to brush her teeth and collect a book to read.

She did brush her teeth, and did pick out a book from the small pile she had bought; then with it and her key in one hand, she was about to open the door with the other when a knock came on it.

Puzzled for a moment, then apprehensive in case it had anything to do with this trouble they had been warned about, she reached for the knob and turned it.

She was neither puzzled nor apprehensive then; she was astounded. She said sharply, 'What are you doing here, Theo? You should be with your mother and. . .' she couldn't bring herself to say Ahmed's name, so continued '. . .and the others at the Middle Oasis.'

'Well, I'm not! I left a note behind saying I was going home.'

'Look, Theo, I'm sorry you're not going out to the desert,' began Leonie, 'and that you're going home, but I truly must go now, Mrs Hailstrom is expecting me.'

'I would like you to come out to a nightclub. . .or even a coffee bar. I'm really glad I met you, Leonie. . .'

Breaking in quickly, Leonie said, 'Of course I'm not going out with you, Theo. Of course I'm not. I wouldn't go chasing round a strange city at night with someone I hardly know—and an Eastern city at that. Don't be silly!' Exasperation coloured her words.

She went to reach behind her to switch out the light, but Theo's hand moved swiftly too. . .to manacle a wrist. 'Just let me come in for a while, Leonie,' he coaxed. 'I want to ask you something.'

Terrified that he might push through the gap she had left and take her into the room with him, she stepped quickly outside and slammed shut the door. 'Now, I'm going, Theo,' she told him curtly.

She wouldn't have thought he was so strong. His

fingers gripping her wrist were biting into her skin. Again she said curtly, 'Let go of my wrist, Theo. You're hurting me!'

'No, because if I do you will go away, and I don't want you to. Please come out with me, Leonie.'

Across his shoulder, she saw the porter at his station glancing at them, and coming down the corridor were two Egyptian businessmen. They too were looking their way. She said again through clenched teeth, 'Let go of me! People are looking.'

'Just come for a little while, I do want to ask you something.'

A group of women tourists emerging from the lifts were walking towards them. They looked at the couple standing before a closed bedroom door, hands seemingly tightly clasped, and smiled as they went past.

I can't hit him, which I'd like to do. Mrs Hailstrom is too well known in this hotel for me to create a scene outside her suite, thought Leonie. So, sighing, she said, 'I'll come up to the roof-garden with you—for five minutes only. Right?'

Having got his own way, Theo smiled widely, nodding. But he kept hold of her wrist until the lift door had closed. As they walked along side by side, hands clasped as lovers would do, Leonie didn't see the porter had been joined by another Arab clad in an enveloping black and silver burnous. There came one sharp question in their own tongue and then both men turned to watch the couple walk the length of the corridor until they entered the lift. She didn't know, either, that the newcomer stood watching the indicator light, then followed upstairs in the next lift.

While up on the roof-garden above the lighted city, her wrist released, Leonie said sharply, 'Now tell me, Theo, what you're really doing here, and why aren't you up at the Middle Oasis?' She stood there rubbing her wrist.

'I came down after you; to do what I wanted to do up in Aswan.' Theo reached out and took hold of her two hands this time, catching them firmly to bring her right up against him.

More angry than frightened, Leonie gazed at the young face so few inches from her own. It held a wide grin, a complacent grin, as he looked down at her. No harshness, no violence showed there; just glee at obtaining what he wanted. . .and at what he intended to do.

He took no notice of the glass door swinging open, or at the three older women who came through, who after one glance at the couple standing so close together, walked over to the parapet.

Leonie did, however. She said through clenched teeth, 'Don't be stupid, Theo. Let me go!'

But those gripping hands were drawing her inexorably nearer to him, his grin growing even wider. Straining backwards against the pull, Leonie thought, I can't make a scene, and this damned boy knows that. Then Theo's head came down, and as it did she swung her own sideways. All she was aware of was anger, not of an Arab enclosed in an enveloping burnous who had come to look through the glass doors, who, after one assessing glance, had turned to move away.

As he did so, Leonie stamped hard with her sandalled heel on the instep of Theo's foot. He cried out, and abruptly one of her hands was free. With it, she pushed, and Theo went tumbling backwards, taking the white metal table and a chair with him.

Three heads turned sharply from gazing out over Cairo, three mouths dropped open as everyone said, 'Oh. . .ooh!' Leonie took no notice. She turned and marched straight-backed through the ante-room and on towards the lifts. She might have hurried a little along the corridor to her employer's room, and she let out a small breath of relief as she closed it behind her and turned the lock.

'I was beginning to worry, Leonie, what with all these warnings about trouble looming. What kept you so long?' Strain sounded through the curtness of Mrs Hailstrom's voice.

'I'm sorry. . .' Leonie sank down on her bed, rubbing a wrist still showing the imprint of Theo's heavy grip. 'But you wouldn't believe what just happened, Mrs Hailstrom,' she said, and went on to tell her about Theo and his behaviour. 'I wouldn't have believed he could act that way with so little encouragement,' she finished.

'Yes, well, Theo has been spoilt—by his guardians, not by Helen. And with a handsome young Greek having money as well. . .' Mrs Hailstrom allowed her words to trail off.

'I can tell you he certainly acted as if he was used to having his own way,' answered Leonie, while hoping she would never see him again. Then, as Mrs Hailstrom climbed into bed and switched off the light, Leonie did the same. Turning her face to the wall, she told herself she was not going to think of Ahmed, and for the first time since she had met him, she didn't.

She didn't know that, when the hotel had been quiet for some hours, an Arab returned to the porter's station. He spoke a sharp sentence in his own language. Keys were picked up, a door unlocked, with the visitor glancing around an empty room; at her case, the skirt hanging on the outside of the wardrobe, the unused bed. Outside again, he went away as before.

* * *

And it was just before seven o'clock, when the hotel was beginning to wake up, that another visitor arrived at the porter's station. No enveloping black and silver burnous covered this figure. In flowing pristine white, but flaunting a black and silver cord around his kaffiyeh, he snapped a curt question to the man who had stood silently there all night. Then a finger was raised, and again a door was opened on an empty room.

That finger lifted for a second time and pointed. It was the next door which was knocked on.

Hearing it, just about to brush her hair, Leonie glanced at Mrs Hailstrom. 'Yes, you get it, Leonie,' she was instructed.

So, dressed in the loose green linen dress she had worn last night, Leonie opened the door. . .and stepped swiftly back, unable to help herself. Then she said carefully to the unsmiling, almost inimical man who stood there, 'Is it Mrs Hailstrom you want?'

He looked at her, once glance which passed over and beyond her, but she knew that that fierce, arrogantly angry gaze from tawny eagle's eyes had seen all it wanted to.

Damn him, she thought, what did she care how he felt about her? He needn't worry about his precious cousin being involved with her. Damn him, she thought again, aware from somewhere inside her that his brief look had carried deep critical scorn.

Mrs Hailstrom was coming along to meet him, saying, 'Why, Hassan!' welcome and affection apparent in the two words.

'I'm going to change,' Leonie told her employer, and began to edge awkwardly past that inimical figure. She thought it seemed just as concerned—if not as awkwardly—to avoid contact with her too.

Angry, furious, she changed into her skirt and

blouse and white working shoes, wondering, why that manner? Even if he knew—and hadn't Ahmed said once that the Wallifa knew everything?—of Ahmed's interest in her, surely that was no reason for such a scornful attitude. She realised that in their eyes she was probably not a suitable person for Ahmed to be serious about, but she *was* a respectable working girl, pleasantly attractive, and she didn't merit those looks. She didn't!

Oh, well, she decided, packing quickly, once I might have been upset about it, but now Sheikh Hassan Wallifa simply doesn't concern me. So, make-up applied, hair combed out of the straggle that man would have seen it in, she picked up her small case and went hesitantly to the next door.

It was shut, and on opening it Leonie found her employer alone inside. Asking no questions, she ran up the zip of the loose dress the other woman was wearing, saying, 'You'll be able to do this yourself soon, won't you? Now, I'll finish packing your case.'

'That would be a help, Leonie, because we have to leave immediately and have breakfast at the airport.'

Answered with only a raised eyebrow, Mrs Hailstrom explained, 'Hassan has a car downstairs and he says we'd do better to go out at once. And don't ask me,' she replied to Leonie's enquiring look, 'what it's all about, because I don't know. . .and neither does he. However, he's finished his business here, closed up their big house and sent his men up to Aswan in the launch. He also said he had had a message from Ahmed for you but that he'd been unable to deliver it.'

'How could he have received such a message? There would be no reason for Ahmed to get in touch with me.'

'Oh, well, it doesn't matter now as we're going home, but. . .' Suddenly that malicious smile which her employer's face sometimes took on surfaced as she said, 'I can just imagine the six fits the old Sheikh Ahmed would have if he knew his precious son and heir had only one man in attendance instead of the usual half a dozen!'

Not wanting to talk about this young man who had looked at her so scornfully, Leonie said, 'There, your case is finished. Now, are we ready?'

Yes, they were ready. Leonie opened the door and went to carry the cases into the hallway, but was stopped by a raised hand. Two porters picked up the cases and, with Leonie carrying her own and Mrs Hailstrom's large handbags, they walked down the corridor to enter the lifts, the Arab in the Wallifa headdress and burnous following behind.

In the large foyer they didn't go near the desk to pay anything so mundane as bills; they joined the white-clad figure waiting for them. It was Leonie who helped her employer into the back seat of the big black anonymous car, while Sheikh Hassan and his attendant stepped into the front beside the driver. And once more Leonie was driving through the busy streets of this city where she had met Ahmed.

CHAPTER ELEVEN

'WHOA there, boy!' Leonie was laughing as she pulled Tarot to a stop. She sat there on the slight rise, patting the shining muscles below her knees, and gazed out over a land which had become familiar to her. Surprised, she heard movement behind and beside her, and looked round. Six men were crowding close, Mohammed remaining outside their circle.

She smiled at Hussein, saying, 'Good evening.'

He bowed slightly, and told her, 'My Lord Ahmed says, will you come with us, please?'

Puzzled, she just gazed at him, wondering if she had heard aright, or if Hussein had made a mistake in his message. But Hussein spoke good English.

'No, I can't come now, Hussein,' she told him pleasantly. 'I have to take Tarot home. Probably the Lord Ahmed will get in touch with me later.'

'No, lady—now! I am to take you to him. Will the lady dismount and ride on the camel?'

More than puzzled, astounded now, Leonie saw that four camels had been brought up. She had not heard them arrive. She hadn't seen camels like them before, either—thin, cream all over, with legs that seemed to go on forever.

She said, more firmly now, even curtly, 'No, I will not come now, Hussein. Mrs Hailstrom will wonder where I am.'

'A message has been sent—she will know. Please, we have to go.'

Beginning to get angry now, Leonie told him just as curtly, '*You* might have to go, Hussein. I do not!'

'Lady, please, come down and mount the camel, or Mahmoud will try to help you.' The words were spoken in Hussein's normal polite tone, but he was gesturing to a tall burly Arab standing well back. Hussein was probably only following orders, but, furiously angry now, Leonie gathered her reins tightly, intending to hit Tarot and ride off. Her bridle was caught and held.

She half raised her whip to slash down on that preventing arm, then stopped herself. It wasn't Hussein's fault. How dared Ahmed put her in this position?

She swung down from the saddle by herself, disdaining any helping hand, and went over to the indicated camel, which was now kneeling. She knew how to mount it, she had been on one—once. But she also knew it wasn't her favourite form of transport. Being swung high as the beast rose, she saw that the six Wallifa men had mounted two to a camel, with only herself riding solo.

Then they were moving, and glancing back, she saw Mohammed accompanied by another Arab leading Tarot away on a rein.

Her leg around the horn of the saddle, she held firmly to the reins and did not glance about her for some minutes. Then, finding she could manage, that she wasn't going to fall off, and that she was not going to be made sick by the swaying motion, she raised her eyes to look around her.

It was only just after five o'clock, she saw with a glance at her watch. The sun would not be sinking for almost an hour yet. She wondered if they would get to where Ahmed was before dark. . .she wondered why camels and not horses!

They were riding swiftly, and, veering slightly now, Leonie saw they were travelling due west. They moved in silence except for an occasional phrase in Arabic which Leonie supposed was directed at the animals. They also rode towards a sun which was sliding down to the horizon more quickly every minute.

Then that vivid crimson orb was gone, descending abruptly beyond the edge of the world. And also abruptly there came to Leonie a different vibration from the padding feet beneath her. They had left the hard ground behind and were riding now on desert sands.

Forgetting herself and her anger for a brief minute, Leonie found delight in the swift movement and magic that twilight was bringing to her surroundings. There were no stars yet, full darkness being still minutes away. But suddenly they were stopping and Hussein was at her side.

He said, holding out a garment towards her, 'It will be cold soon, lady. You will need this.'

Glancing across at that young face, Leonie saw only the willingness to please which she had always had from him. But also coming from the cloak he was holding out came an aroma of sandalwood. Of course, something belonging to Ahmed. Hot anger came again at the way she had summarily been accosted and brought against her will without so much as a note from him, and she thought astringently that she would be damned if she would wear it. She shook her head, saying, 'No, I don't want it,' and as Hussein still tried to press it on her, she pushed it away with the riding whip still hanging by a thong around her wrist.

Her second 'No!' was sharper as again he told her,

'It will be cold, lady.' Then as her face remained still turned stubbornly from him, Hussein moved aside and uttered a sharp exclamation.

It was faster than riding a galloping horse, Leonie decided as the shouted command sent their animals flying. Sent time flying too as black darkness crowded about them.

She began to feel cold, but she was still glad she had refused that cloak. She would rather freeze and fall off! And she thought, what seemed aeons later, that she might well freeze and fall off if this nightmare journey didn't soon end.

They seemed to have been riding for hours, and once again she gazed up at a sky of deep black. . .and at the empty, unfamiliar desert all about her. She rubbed one arm and then the other, one leg and then the other, trying to bring warmth into them.

Then stars low down on the horizon were coming into view. Not white, brilliant stars like those above; these were blazing with a soft orange tinge, and they were coming closer. So they appeared at last to be coming to what she thought must be their destination. Converging upon it, she saw the outline of palms, of buildings and tents.

Then the camels were brought to a halt, but two of them only were kneeling, the other two padding away, and as soon as Hussein had dismounted, the third one followed. They had come to a halt before a very large tent, which appeared to be surrounded by palm trees, and from which bright light was spilling into the night through a hooked-back tent flap.

Leonie looked down at Hussein standing beside her mount, then glanced round, expecting to see Ahmed, wondering in her anger what she would say to him. He wasn't there.

As Hussein still stood waiting, she freed both legs and slid down. She found she had to lean back against the shoulder of her camel, legs cramped from the long ride, body shaking with cold.

'Through here, lady,' said her guide. So she turned, walking unsteadily, and moving through the uplifted flap found she was almost blinded by the brightness within. Still hugging her arms against herself for warmth, she gazed round. At a table and two chairs at one end of the big room, and at the other. . . She brought her back straighter, letting her arms fall, violent anger careering through her.

Ahmed was there! Dressed in loosely fitting white and smoking a small black cigarillo which she had seen him do once before—or as she had smelt it once before as it was thrown, a red spark arching into the night from the veranda railing of her room. He was sitting on a couch listening to a radio from which was issuing the excited voice of an announcer. He reached over and flicked a switch.

In the silence of that closed-in space, he turned to look at her across the distance separating their two figures. Then he was rising and walking slowly over the thickly carpeted floor.

As he didn't speak, Leonie did. 'Will you tell me, please,' she began, knowing that her voice was shaking from both anger at his attitude and from cold. And when he didn't answer, she repeated, 'Would you tell me, please, why you've had me come all this way out here in this unexpected fashion? Without the courtesy of coming properly to even ask me. . .'

'I have had you brought here because I wanted to do so. Does that answer your question?'

Aghast at that tone, those words, from this so different Ahmed, Leonie found she couldn't answer for a moment, then she said, 'I don't understand why you're acting like this!' All the anger which she had been feeling on that long ride disentegrated. Somehow she was frightened. But even if she had decided to go home after her rebuttal in that moonlit desert, this was the Ahmed whom she had loved. . . She pulled her thoughts into order and said again, 'Why have you had me brought here in this fashion?'

'Surely you don't mind?' said that grating silken voice. 'You have shown me on other occasions that you are not averse to my presence. . .or even to my lovemaking.'

She knew that the burning flush which had run upwards couldn't stain her cheeks—they were too cold. She made herself face him directly, forcing herself to reply. 'Yes, to my sorrow you have reason to say such things. But now, if you don't mind, I would like to go home.'

'But I must inform you, my dear Leonie, that what you wish or don't wish has no bearing at all on the situation.'

She couldn't believe those words, she couldn't understand the way he was acting. He wasn't drunk; there was not the slightest slur to his voice. Her glance went to the small dark cigarillo he was still holding between long brown fingers. Could some drug he was smoking cause this behaviour? She said bleakly, 'Mrs Hailstrom is certainly wrong in her assessment of you, in the way she thinks of you. I must tell her so when I return.'

'You can certainly do that, if you feel like telling her about the next two days. . .and nights. Oh, yes, I imagine two days—and of course the nights—will suffice.'

So close to her, he raised a finger to run it across the

frown indented between her brows. His finger lifted abruptly, and he placed the palm of his hand against her cheek.

His next words were an exclamation in Arabic. Then he said in English, 'You're cold. . .nearly frozen! I thought you were shaking with anger. Weren't you given a warm cloak?'

Before she could answer, he had swung round to the open tent-flap with a question erupting sharply. She heard Hussein answer, and found she couldn't stop shaking—and it wasn't only from cold. Then Ahmed had turned back, standing away from her, smoking.

Being unnerved by that look from half-closed eyes— eyes she had not seen properly open since she arrived—Leonie went to speak. But a hand flicking sideways bade her to be silent. Then a young girl was entering, and Ahmed said, 'Go with Zanaide and she will provide you with hot water. We will eat when you return.'

His hand moved again, and the pretty dark girl went swiftly past through the hooked-back curtain. Leonie made no attempt to follow her. She said carefully, 'I am not going in there to wash. I am not going to stay! I want to go back to Aswan!'

Ahmed was abruptly close to her, his cigarillo discarded. One hand clasped her arm tightly, the other began to unbutton the check cotton shirt she wore. 'It is immaterial to me,' he told her in that grating silken voice, 'if I have to undress you myself here or if you go and allow Zanaide to help you. Because, believe me, I intend to enjoy myself tonight—and enjoying myself with a frozen body will not amuse me. Now, we can do it in a civilised way. . .or any other way you can desire.'

The first button unfastened, he began on the second one.

'You *are* mad!' exclaimed Leonie, and tried to pull away.

But the clasp on her arm gripped more tightly, bringing pain. From inches away she suddenly saw lids lift from the green eyes, and found she was looking into a gaze of molten heat. Unable to help herself, she recoiled. . .and heard Ahmed laugh.

'No, I am not mad,' he told her. 'I am just angry at myself for being such a simpleton. . .and with you for appearing as you did, while being the promiscuous adventuress that you are.'

'Promiscuous? You *are* mad!' Was this all because she had shown him so plainly that she was his for the taking—which he would have known, of course he would, man of the world that he was. But it was only to him that she had behaved so; always only to him.

She said now, bleakly, 'If you're not mad, then you must be smoking hashish or some such thing—to act and speak like this. Please, I do want to go back to Mrs Hailstrom.'

Again that harsh laugh from deep within his throat erupted. And, looking at the face from which it came, she noticed the change in it. It wasn't pale—of course it wasn't, with his ancestry. But the sculptured countenance she had once compared to that of a Greek marble statue looked different. The cheekbones appeared more prominent, the full lips thinner. Then as that austere figure's hand reached out once again, Leonie nodded and turned towards the inner room. What else could she do?

She found herself pushed gently into a chair, with her ankle-length desert boots being pulled off; she found herself guided through a thick plastic curtain and sat on a chair. In a daze, shivering still, she was divested of jeans and shirt, bra and briefs, and gently helped to stand up again.

She gasped as hot water was poured from a jug over her cold body, then turned under it, thawing rapidly under the warm life-giving jet. Then small hands enveloped her in a large towel. Gestured to return to the bedroom, but more herself now, she pushed away the hand endeavouring to dry her, saying, 'I can manage.'

She told herself that she couldn't help it if this towel too reminded her of Ahmed, but when Zanaide held out a loose white garment towards her, she looked at it and shook her head, saying, 'No!'

Casting a quick look towards the hooked-back curtain, the young girl said, 'You must, lady. The Lord Ahmed has ordered it.' Then with another glance at Leonie's set face, she said apprehensively, 'The Lord Ahmed has been angry all day. It doesn't often happen, but when it does, we all do as we are told, quickly—and at once! You *must* put this on and go out to eat.'

'Where are my own clothes?' Leonie's voice was not so definite as it had been when saying her 'No.' Zanaide did seem frightened. And she too felt a little fearful when remembering her reception and the things that had been said. It *was* a different man outside from the one she had known.

'They have been taken away to be cleaned. Here, lady.' The thin muslin gown was held out to her once more.

Again wondering what else could she do, Leonie slipped her arms through the sleeves, and thought with a curl of her lips that it must be what that man wore.

Like an old-fashioned kimono, it fell open all the way down, and of course would wrap round her twice over.

Zanaide glanced at her for a moment, looked around, then went to a large cedar chest. She returned with something that was very familiar. Pulling the large garment tightly around Leonie, she bound it firmly about the waist with a black and silver cord, then smiled as at work well done.

Remaining in the same place, rubbing absently at hair just beginning to dry a little, Leonie was slow in taking the comb held out to her. 'You must hurry, lady,' came the quick words from Zanaide. So perforce she combed the damp hair into its usual style around her clean-washed face and, taking a deep necessary breath, walked through the opening and into the other room, Zanaide following.

It wasn't as brightly lit as it had been the last time she had seen it. The centre overhead light was extinguished, leaving only a side one to cast its illumination over a table on wiich food was being placed. Leonie saw steam rising from dishes a servant was checking on a trolley, then he had bowed his head slightly and was moving away. He didn't cast the slightest glance in Leonie's direction.

Neither did Ahmed for a moment. He walked over and unhooked the tent-flap, allowing it to fall solidly into place. Then he was turning, and Leonie found herself on the receiving end of a comprehensive glance that roved all over her. She felt her face burn.

'Looking at you now,' said a voice which held none of the easy, pleasant tone she had come to associate with Ahmed, 'I am coming to realise that I can't blame myself as much as I have been doing. You could be an innocent sixteen. . .and how damned deceptive that impression is!. . .but thank Allah I have been shown what folly can be made of, and am now in my right senses.'

Not understanding him, she went to speak, but Ahmed flipped a hand, indicating a chair. Just as he does to his servants and knows absolutely that he'll be obeyed! thought Leonie rebelliously. Nevertheless, she moved across to the indicated seat. She wasn't hungry, she knew, even if they had had an early lunch on arriving home from Cairo, and that it was very late for dinner now. She also knew it was only nerves, but still nerves had to be taken into consideration.

A long brown hand placed a soup bowl before her, and Ahmed said, 'Eat.'

Leonie picked up her spoon, but made no effort to carry it further, then the man opposite said in a tone that grated on all those nerves she had just thought about, 'I told you before it was immaterial to me if you allowed Zanaide to help you or not. I am telling you now it is also immaterial to me if you would rather not eat, thus enabling us to adjourn to the next room at once.'

Leonie dipped her spoon into the liquid before her. She found it was delicious—and hot, and she drank it all. But with the main course being placed before her, she discovered she was unable to touch it. She thirstily drank the tea she was served.

Thinking of his behaviour, simply not understanding it, and yes, angry too, she said, 'Greg was right when he warned me about you. Everything he told me has come exactly true!'

She wasn't prepared for the violent anger that made his chair go back with a rush—or the scorching chagrin looking out at her from blazing emerald eyes. She wasn't prepared either for the words that issued through lips thinned to almost white lines. 'Don't tell me,' he said, 'don't you dare tell me that you discussed me with Coughlan! Before heaven, I could kill you! But then again, there are other ways that are open to me, and as Allah is my judge I am going to use all of them.'

'I. . . I don't know what you're talking about,' Leonie was stammering. 'I didn't discuss you with Greg. I've never discussed you with anyone! It. . .it was the day I arrived in Cairo, and. . .and you were at the airport. On the way to the hospital I asked Greg about all of you. He told me that although I didn't come under his Embassy's protection, he would still give me the advice he gave to his own—and that was that Arab princes and sheikhs were not people to get involved with, no matter what one read to the contrary. . .'

'It's too bad, then, isn't it, that you didn't heed his advice?' interrupted Ahmed.

'Yes, it is. Because it was only you I was interested in. . . Not the Prince, or even Hassan later on. . .'

Ahmed's fist thumped on the table and dishes rattled. 'Don't mention Hassan to me! Do you think I enjoyed what my more than cousin. . .' White-faced, he stood up, and, really frightened at the force and black anger in his words, Leonie did the same.

She was pushed before him into the other room, which in its turn had its curtain untied and dropped to the floor; and so they stood together confined in a closeness of dimly lighted space.

He moved a step nearer, and Leonie backed away. Then, as in the first room, he gripped her arm, holding her to him as his head came down. He said, his lips just above her own, 'You mustn't mind if I don't use courtesy and grace which once I would have done in the act of making love between us. Because I've discovered that that is not necessary. So tonight. . .now, I can allow all my need and desire to take whatever course it finds its way along.'

Panic-stricken, not understanding those offensive words flung so carelessly at her, Leonie opened her mouth to protest. All objections were smothered as his lips came down on her own, caressing her with slow kisses that brought their own response from her. After all, this *was* Ahmed. The brown handsome face lifted—only a fraction—and deep within his throat, Ahmed laughed mockingly as he said, 'Do you respond to all your lovers so satisfyingly with the first kiss?' and, picking her up, he swung her on the turned-down bed.

With the heavy body so close along her side, one arm crushed beneath him, the other held loosely by the wrist above her head, Leonie still couldn't see his face. His head was downbent, gazing intently at what his fingers were doing.

He said, 'I didn't know this thing had other uses as well as adorning my kaffiyeh; but it has served its purpose here as it does there.' The black and silver cord was now unfastened and thrown carelessly aside. One long finger moved slowly and set apart the soft white muslin, then travelled down the bare silken skin it had exposed. Leonie closed her eyes.

She said, 'Don't, Ahmed! It's not right. . .'

Again came that grating laugh. 'Oh, yes,' said Ahmed slurringly, 'it *is* right, that I should have what I have now; what I have desired and never taken before—and which I am going to enjoy very much from this moment on. I *could* be sorry that from necessity I might not be as tender and caring this first time, but we have all night for me to remedy that. . .and by then I might be able to send us to paradise, taking hour after hour in making love.'

His head came down to rest lips on her throat. Her head turned aside as far as she could manage, Leonie thought that although this love of hers was turning into a nightmare, she wasn't going to cry. . .or plead! She wasn't.

Then those searching lips moved upwards, and, while resting on her cheek, paused. Then Ahmed was up on an elbow, his face looking down at her in the dimness. A brown finger came out and brushed lightly, and his voice, so low Leonie could hardly hear it, said, 'Tears, Leonie? Does my presence call for these tears I can feel?'

Making herself speak, Leonie said, 'I don't understand why you're behaving like this. Is it because I was angry with you after that desert ride?'

Ahmed's voice answered, and it carried no softness now; it spoke sharply in Arabic. His weight departed from her side as he reached out to pull the chain of the bedlamp. Up further on an elbow now, he gazed down upon her.

'Why did you spend last night with young Paulus?' he asked.

'*What*?' she exclaimed, and then again, 'What did you say?'

'You heard what I said!'

'Yes, I did hear what you said. But I don't understand it.'

Then suddenly, like being left in the eye of a cyclone, the raging storm was gone. The room was eerily quiet, no sound from outside penetrating, only the ragged breathing of the man beside her sounded in the stillness.

Ahmed took the four pillows and packed them

against the low headrest, then clasping her under the arms, he lifted her to lean against them. He bent down and brought the top sheet to spread across her, then he said, 'Now, you are going to tell me why I have been informed that you didn't spend last night in your room at Shepheards.' The tone of his voice now was neither easy or pleasant. . .or like grating silk. It was bleak and authoritative.

'Now tell me,' he said again, 'where you spent last night,' and continued curtly as she remained silent, 'Because if you don't, we can start again where we've just left off, and believe me, that would entail no hardship for me. . . Now, I was informed that you spent last night in Cairo with young Paulus. . .all night. You never returned to your room!'

Leonie's lip curled. 'I didn't realise I had spies set on me—oh!' she exclaimed suddenly, understanding, 'I suppose it was Hassan. Well, thank goodness, I won't have to meet him—or you—again. Because after this episode, I expect to be taken home at daybreak tomorrow. And Greg was right—you are both desert barbarians!'

'You haven't answered my question. Where did you spend last night?' The words came out like drops of iced water.

'Where I spent it is none of your business!' Her teeth clenched on her lower lip, and she blinked away tears that were gathering again.

'You are mistaken—it is very much my business. Now, where did you spend last night?'

She made herself look directly at him, at that hard, ruthless countenance, and her own face showed hurt and distress. She moved restlessly.

The tense, indented lines on Ahmed's face deepened, but he only said again, 'Where did you spend last night?'

She knew she would have to tell him. So she decided to get it all over and done with. She said baldly, 'I spent it in Mrs Hailstrom's room!'

"Why would you do that? You had a perfectly good room of your own.'

'Yes, but you remember we were warned there was going to be trouble. Mrs Hailstrom thought it best that we were together.' Leonie sighed. She wanted to get out of this bed; to get away from that long brown body lying so close to her. So, with the dim silent room all about them, she explained how last night had brought about that whole comedy of errors.

At last finished, she threw out a hand as Ahmed went to answer her. She said, 'I don't want to know. All I want to do is go home—first to Aswan and then to Australia. Please. . .after you've been proved so wrong, you owe me that, Ahmed.'

He heard the plea; he turned from her and lay flat, so she quickly pushed aside the sheet and slipped out of the bed, pulling the muslin gown about her.

She went over to the dressing-table and began to brush her hair, then wondered what she was doing. She dropped the brush and turned back to look at him. He was holding out the black and silver cord which he had earlier undone. His eyebrow went up, asking if she would use it.

'Why not?' she replied, taking it from him. All she wanted to do was wipe that previous hour from her memory, to do and say only ordinary things until she could get away from this place. So she took the cord.

Ahmed asked, 'Will you have something to eat, Leonie? You didn't. . .'

She turned on him, aghast. 'You must be mad, Ahmed, thinking I can go out there and just eat! I only want you to leave me alone until I can be taken home.'

'Yes, all right! But you haven't eaten, and. . .'

'I'm not going to eat. I've told you. . .' Then, gazing at that hard, ruthless face, she said in a very different tone, 'I don't want to, and there's nothing now that you can threaten me with!'

Ahmed laughed aloud. She couldn't believe it. It held amusement deep within its very cadence. 'Oh, I think there could be,' came the soft reply.

And suddenly, from thinking nothing he could ever say again would make her blush, Leonie felt a tide of burning colour stain her cheeks. Oh, yes, there was something he could threaten her with.

'I called through and ordered tea and toast to be brought in,' that soft voice was issuing from a face which showed no softness at all—only the ruthlessness of determination. 'It sounds,' continued Ahmed, 'as if it has just arrived.'

Leonie looked past his shoulder, and the big bed was in her vision. She knew she wouldn't be taken home tonight; she also knew she wouldn't sleep. So she supposed that was as good a way as any other to pass the time.

She walked past him into the big living-room. The tea and toast *had* arrived. The servant had set down a tray. He turned, nodded to Ahmed, looked past Leonie as if she wasn't there, and departed.

The toast was hot and soft with melted butter. Leonie pushed it aside with a shudder, and poured tea.

'Don't be stupid, Leonie. Eat it. Faisal has gone to enormous trouble to see that it is appetising.'

Astounded by the tone, and more so at the words, Leonie thought that the man Faisal wouldn't even know what she looked like. She put the toast to her mouth—and ate it all, both pieces.

Ahmed was standing at the tent opening, gazing out into the night, and as a shadow moved towards him, there came the sound of quiet voices speaking in Arabic. Then back inside, Ahmed pulled the other chair from the table and sat sideways to it.

Teacup held in both hands, Leonie remained there wondering how she could broach the subject of leaving. She asked him instead, 'Was there trouble in Cairo? The announcer over the radio sounded very excited.'

'Yes, there *was* trouble in Cairo, but it was a bloody misfortune that you had to be there on that one day. That one damned day! And also that we had to hear the rumours about it. All we wanted to do was keep you off the streets. As it happened, it wouldn't have mattered. The affair would never have come near you.'

'Yes, it was unfortunate,' Leonie replied tiredly, then added, 'We'll have to leave before daybreak if we're to get through the desert before it's too hot, won't we?' She decided the tone of her voice was sensible, her words careful, carrying no umbrage.

'Look, Leonie, we'll talk about that in the morning. For now, I have something you might take. It will help you sleep. It is a native mixture made up by our women.'

Alarmed, Leonie said immediately, 'No! No, I don't want anything like that!'

'Just as you like. If I had such a thing as a sleeping pill, I would offer you one, but I'm afraid my medicine cabinet only rises to such Western remedies as pain-killers for broken bones and their like. Still, whatever you want to do?' One black eyebrow rose as he gazed at her. He looked tired.

Suddenly she remembered all the times he had been charming, all the places to which he had taken her—none of which could ever make up for the way he had behaved tonight—but still. . .

'Yes, thank you, I will take it,' she said. 'I wouldn't like not being able to sleep tonight.'

Ahmed turned away abruptly so that she didn't see the tiny smile of satisfaction that this small concession had brought. He got up and, pouring a small glass full of a grey liquid, brought it across to her.

Upending it, Leonie swallowed the lot, then hurriedly reached for her tea-cup, saying, 'Ugh!'

Ahmed asked then in the polite conversational voice he was using, 'Would you like to sit for a while over on the couch? I haven't any Western music here, but you might like some of my native recordings.'

'Yes, I think I might,' said Leonie thankfully, knowing she didn't want to enter that room behind her. She felt also no effect whatsoever from that glass of liquid she had drunk, so she walked the few yards to where her companion was straightening cushions, and sat down, leaning against them.

Ahmed did put on music. . .very low, then sat on the carpet out of her sight. He asked her quietly about the music she had liked to listen to at home.

She was telling him, explaining that she liked some pop, some musical comedy also, at one minute; the next she was deeply unconscious. Waiting a moment until a question remained unanswered, Ahmed rose from his position on the carpet and bending over her, said, 'Leonie. . .'

When no reply was forthcoming, he swung the sleeping figure into his arms and carrying her through into the other room, laid her on the bed. He leant down and once again that night unfastened the tight cord around her waist, allowing it to lie there loosely about her.

The soft muslin slipped from her thigh, leaving apricot-tinted flesh exposed. Ahmed's face took on an even more austere look as he pulled up the sheet and quilt to carefully cover the supine form.

Then, walking over to the dressing-table, he lit the wick of a small oil lamp which had been used in this country for a thousand years, and, pulling down the chain of the bedside lamp, plunged the room into a darkness illuminated by only a small glow from the just recently ignited flame. He walked from the room.

CHAPTER TWELVE

ALL around was a quietness that seemed strange, Leonie thought as she curled up drowsily under the covers. It wasn't a noisy house, this almost palace of Mrs Hailstrom's, but it did usually have the sounds of an awakening residence preparing for a new day.

She decided she had better get up and see how her employer's exercises were going. That thought penetrating, Leonie stretched. . .and remembered where she was. She could see no one in the room, so she sat up. That mixture Ahmed had given her should be patented, she thought. She had gone out like a light, and felt no after-effects this morning.

But she would leave this morning, and forget about Egypt and the people she had met there, she decided firmly.

Apparently seeing her move, Zanaide came across to the bed. 'Good morning, lady,' she said, smiling. 'Will you please wash and get dressed? Breakfast is waiting outside.'

Leonie looked at the girl, but no other expression except the wish to be helpful showed, so she slid out of bed, and walked across the thickly carpeted floor to the bathroom area.

Pushing all extraneous thoughts away, vowing not to think of Ahmed, or last night, until she was away from this place, Leonie washed, dressed with relief in her own clothes, clean and waiting for her, then, head held high, she walked out to greet Ahmed. He wasn't there.

Her breakfast was. She ate it, boiled eggs, toast, the lot. Then as if he had been waiting for that moment—or more likely been apprised of it—Ahmed came through the open tent-flap. Looking across at him, Leonie willed her face to show nothing, her body to remain sitting still, anchored to the chair.

He came across to her, the tall handsome man dressed in khaki shirt and trousers. With sleeves rolled up above his elbows he was a working man. No flowing white was in evidence today. Sitting on a chair he pulled sideways, he asked her, 'Leonie, will you please listen carefully to what I have to say? I realise that you may not want to, but it is necessary. Now, do you know anything about the Greek church?'

Astounded at such a subject being mentioned, Leonie told him, 'No, not very much, although I had some Greek friends in the outback who sometimes used our church.'

'Thank God for that!' Thank God, she noticed, not thank Allah. But Ahmed was continuing, 'I have been on the phone all morning, and we can be married in the Greek church in Cairo tomorrow evening. We will go directly across country to the river and pick up the launch there, which will save time. . .'

Leonie's hand went up to interrupt this flow of words, her own words completing the process. 'I said last night at one particular time that I thought you were mad. I'll say it again, Ahmed. I'm not going to marry you—in the Greek church or any other place. I'm not!'

'I'm afraid you are, Leonie. You might think now that you don't want to. . .and heaven knows you have reason for that attitude because of what I thought about you, and then behaved the way I did. But I'm afraid you have no choice.'

'Oh, yes, I do have a choice! Last night was last night. But today is today, and you can't make me stand up in front of a priest to say the words that would marry me to you. Even you, a paramount Sheikh of the Wallifa, can't make me do that!'

'I'm afraid,' for the third time this morning Ahmed used the word afraid as he continued, 'that I can, Leonie. To have brought a young girl here and kept her in my quarters all night, when there was no reason for such behaviour on my part, will go all through the encampments of the Wallifa. And it will become known that there was a misunderstanding as far as your behaviour is concerned. My father will be furious, and I won't like that at all. . .

'So. . .you can either come to Cairo and marry me, or I will take you out to one of my own far oases. It will be the same then as if we were married. Now, we are leaving immediately—either to catch the launch, or start for the oasis. The camels are already waiting. It rests with you which way we go.'

Leonie put out a pleading hand, and said, 'Look, Ahmed, this is being silly. Who'll care at home if I've spent the night here—even if it did become known? It's a way of life in Australia—sharing houses and flats.'

'It is not a way of life here, however, I'll have you know. . .and you're wasting time. I'll give you a promise, though. Later on, after all this has settled down, I could be able to give you a divorce—but for now you will marry me!'

'No, I won't!'

'That's where you're mistaken! Now, give me your decision. I don't want to be travelling in the heat of the day, so we leave at once.'

'I don't care. I am not going to Cairo to marry you, Ahmed. I just am not. You're not being fair!'

'Very well then, you're already dressed, you've eaten, so we'll go. You won't mind riding this camel, it belongs to the racing breed that you rode last night.'

'The way you speak, the things you do, I could very well hate riding a camel. . .but what would you care?' Leonie knew she was being childish, but she couldn't help herself. She stood there gazing at the face opposite that showed only the hardness of determination—it could have been chiselled from cold marble.

Stammering, she said, 'Please, I don't want to do this. Please, I want to go home.'

'Look, Leonie, we'll see what the future brings, shall we? Come on, now, you will find that things will sort themselves out.' Suddenly Ahmed's voice had changed from demand, and was coaxing. But the lines about his mouth were still drawn tight, and he said in that soft silken tone she didn't like, 'Look, Leonie, I've put a proposition to you, but I *could* do something else you wouldn't like at all.'

Yes, he could, she knew. 'Very well,' she told him, 'I'll do as you ask, but I have a condition to make.'

'Yes!' Only the one curt word answered her, and she didn't notice the deep relief that was behind it.

'I will marry you. I will come back here until such time as we do sort things out, but I want to be left completely alone.'

'Very well, I will give you that promise—except that I too have a condition to make. I will keep that promise until, or unless, you show me that you want it broken.'

'What do I do now, laugh? You know I only want to go home, so I'll tell you something, Ahmed. You have your own and Buckley's chance of that ever happening!' She walked across then to collect her small whip and soft hat which Zanaide had left on a coffee table.

The hat was taken out of her hand and a white cloak with a hood was draped round her. 'This will be more suitable,' said her companion's voice from above her.

He stood back while she walked outside before him. Guided by the tips of his fingers on her shirt-covered arm, she saw that Ahmed's quarters were apart and surrounded by thickly growing palms. She also saw that the camels were waiting further along in shade and that there seemed a great many of them.

A khaki-clad arm indicated that she go to a camel already kneeling, and, forgetting for the moment all the trauma and anger that had passed between them, Leonie asked, 'Is this the one I rode last night?'

'Yes, she is. And feel honoured—not everybody is allowed to ride her.' Then, as he used to do—and hadn't last night—Ahmed waited beside her mount as she stepped up as she had been taught to do, and was seated.

Passing through an oasis which was much larger than she had thought such a place could be, with a cloud of dust showing horses being worked on the far side, she asked the man riding beside her, 'What is it you breed here, horses or camels?'

'Horses! These,' Ahmed made a throwaway gesture to the swiftly moving beasts carrying them, 'are here to be rested before being transshipped to Jordan.'

'Oh!' Leonie had heard of Jordan's élite Camel Corps. But as her glance roved the speeding animals, she thought that although these were special, the beauty of horses would have her vote any time; but then she had been brought up among horses. Suddenly she looked again. Every man around them had a rifle slung across his back. She turned, glancing across at Ahmed.

He answered her as if she had already spoken. 'We will be riding through country that doesn't belong to us, so. . .'

In her most sarcastic tone, Leonie said sweetly, 'Oh, I was under the impression that everything and everywhere belonged to you. . .certainly in the desert.'

Ahmed laughed, not the silent doubled-up laughter that sometimes issued from him. This was loud and carefree.

I've never heard him laughing like that, thought Leonie. But then with us, on some occasions time was the essence, at others. . . Oh, dear, she thought, and she was suddenly in Ahmed's arms; that Ahmed who hadn't even liked her.

'What's the matter, Leonie? Leonie. . .!' The man riding beside her called sharply.

With an effort she pulled herself together and even dredged up a strained smile. 'What do you mean? Nothing's the matter.' She nudged her animal to get ahead, but of course Ahmed kept pace.

Deliberately dismissing his presence, Leonie gazed around her, knowing that at any other time she would be happily enjoying this ride. An empty desert stretched all around them as far as she could see. Dunes, not flat sand, rose and fell before and around their progress. She knew they were travelling swiftly; she felt it in the vibrations reaching up to her from the quickly padding hooves.

But now she shifted a little, to pull one open side of the cloak up round her face, tucking it in under the hood so that only her eyes were showing. Imitating a yashmak or not, she could imagine what this brilliant, scorching sun would do to a fair skin exposed to it hour by hour.

Her thoughts absently on this, feeling a strange sensation of being observed, she glanced quickly round. Across the small space which Ahmed was only allowing between them at all times, he was looking at her. . .he was laughing at her. 'You look exactly now what people think our women look like, but don't!' he told her.

'I wasn't trying to look like anyone. I was only trying to protect my skin. It's not my fault if I'm riding in blazing heat with none of the sun-screen or oil which I would normally use.'

'You manage very well at everything, I always notice. . .' Ahmed was laughing, speaking naturally to her through it, when abruptly his face closed up, tension tightening the lines around his lips. It was he now who sent his camel a few paces ahead.

He was suddenly thinking of last night, thought Leonie. Will that time always blight his memories of us, as it does with me? she wondered.

But Ahmed's attention was being now claimed by one of the outriders. He nodded at the words spoken to him, then shook his head. Their pace didn't alter.

They covered the countless miles across a desert waste of undulating sand; they rode beneath a scorching deep cobalt sky. Others rode also, moving parallel to their party—but they didn't join them.

When Leonie was beginning to think that even her stamina was wearing thin, a low smudge showed itself on the horizon. It turned, as they got nearer, into vegetation.

The river was there, and so was the launch. It sent its small dinghy put-putting towards them, and before she knew it, she found herself seated on one of the cross-planks, hearing Ahmed giving orders to a bearded man who was most likely a shekih too. Then as the whole party turned, riding away with a long call in Arabic echoing back, he dropped down beside her, with Hussein and Mustafa following.

And once again she was sailing on the blue waters of the Nile.

Leaning against the railing of the launch as it edged from the jetty and began to gather speed, Leonie turned sideways and smiled. There was Shepheards in all its glory, its lighted windows outlining it like a Christmas tree, and further along was the Hilton and other great hotels greeting the night with their brilliance.

How different this return up-river was going to be from the journey down, when all they had done then was travel as rapidly as the launch would take them. She had spent most of that time under a canvas canopy, enveloped in a lethargic haze, just gazing out at the life of southern Egypt going on around her.

Ahmed, who was her husband now, was giving orders to a servant, but as she glanced up she saw his tall figure coming towards her. She smiled at him, this man who had made the strange, half known, half unknown ceremony they had just participated in an occasion of beauty and solemnity she would not have believed possible.

Earlier this afternoon, with the sun descending more swiftly every minute to the horizon, they had disembarked from the launch to enter a familiar black limousine. Ahmed had sat silently in his own corner, yards away from her, until their vehicle had pulled up before an unadorned brick wall with only a large solid wooden gate breaking its stark exterior.

Inside, it was a different matter, the place seemingly more of a palace than even the Hailstrom residence. Leonie had remarked tartly on this fact. 'I had other visions of what a house used by all the Wallifa would be like—and this is certainly not what it was,' she said.

'Oh, but you must remember, Leonie,' that soft voice from above her head had said, 'that my step-mother is a noble from Saudi Arabia. Redecorating our houses is one of her hobbies.'

Was he laughing at her? Of course he was; this Ahmed who was so different from either of the other two she had known. The one she had first met, with always that silken thread of desire drawing them together; the other. . .that frightening, violent one of two nights ago who had shown himself in a silent, tented room. This one was pleasant always, but remote always. And he was still remote while telling her as they walked the exquisitely tile-inlaid corridor, 'I have had clothes sent around which,' here, his glance ran over her as impersonally as a sales assistant's would, 'I expect will fit you. Select what you would like. A dress for the ceremony, and some outdoor clothes for the Oasis. Oh, and. . .' for just the one brief moment that wicked, glinting look had leapt out at her from magnetic emerald eyes, before he'd continued, 'I have also had a beautician from one of the hotel's boutiques come along with that face cream I forgot yesterday.' He *was* laughing at her this time, she knew, even if his face with that new austere look appeared sombre.

Beginning to answer as astringently as she knew how, she had stopped as her companion reached out to open a door, then as he half turned as if to depart, she'd said, and the tartness had carried, 'If I had my own clothes, my own things, that wouldn't be necessary.'

'I have spoken to Mrs Hailstrom and your possessions will be at the Oasis when we return. But we will be four days on the launch going back. And playing the tourist scrambling around tombs and temples, you will need those casual clothes, and your sun-screen, so. . .'

His words had passed over her as another thought intruded. 'Oh, dear. . .what will Mrs Hailstrom say to me?' Leonie had wailed.

'She will say nothing to you. I've told you—I've already spoken to her. . . Look, I have a thousand things to see to and I must go.' Still, over a shoulder as he was turning he'd told her, 'Pick something nice for the ceremony.'

So she had picked something nice for that service she had just participated in, and now she glanced down at the deep ivory crêpe that swung just below her knees. Apparently short dresses were to be the fashion this spring and summer. Ahmed had come to stand beside her now, and they stood, a tall dark man in a cream tropical suit, and a young fair girl in her swirling ivory dress.

They watched the banks of the Nile, dressed in their glittering lights, slide past. Soon, only an occasional fluttering of orange brightness showed that civilisation was still there.

Ahmed turned. Leonie had heard nothing, but apparently the keener hearing of her companion had. A servant had come to stand before them, and Leonie smiled at him. She didn't speak, knowing he had no English, but her companion did, and, receiving a reply, laughed. Standing back, indicating that she go before him, Ahmed told her, 'Suleiman says he hopes you will eat the dinner he has prepared for us—not leave it as you did on the way down.'

Looking at neither of the men, Leonie told the empty space before her, 'Yes, I will. Dare I say that I'm starving?'

'I hope that's true, but I don't believe it. However, we will go and see.'

So they sat under the canopy erected up forward, and as the night passed, Leonie did eat some of the food presented to her—strange food. But when she asked Ahmed what it consisted of, all he said was, 'I wouldn't know, I eat what Suleiman serves me.'

Eating slowly, hearing only the murmur of the water as the ship eased her way through it, Leonie asked him absently, 'Do you always have things done for you, Ahmed? Don't you work at all?'

There came a sharp ejaculation in Arabic. Then, in English, he said forcefully, 'You should see me breaking in our horses. . .and out in the desert trying to improve our water supply. . .and the damned worst thing of all, juggling with books and figures. Oh, for the good old days when our only wealth was in horses and camels—and rifles, when fighting was a way of life.'

'Have you ever fought, Ahmed?' asked Leonie, thinking somehow that she couldn't see him fighting in a modern war—but in a desert one, that was a different matter.

'No!' Abruptly Ahmed was serious. 'The Wallifa are desert Arabs and my uncle keeps a tight hold on them. He is a fierce old man, a real desert chieftain, but I believe you could like him, Leonie.'

'I'll probably never meet him,' said Leonie, hoping that fact would be true. She and Ahmed were acting politely as if guests travelling together, but she didn't want to return to the Oasis; she really didn't want to be anywhere close to him. She would have liked to have been allowed to go to the airport and fly home. Still, she would be doing that in a few weeks and could then begin to get her life together—take out that night, look at it as she couldn't make herself do now, then put it away for ever.

Laying down her fork, pushing the plate away, Leonie picked up her wine glass. Moving a little away from the table, she told her companion, 'I've eaten enough—will you tell Suleiman I enjoyed it, and will he keep some of that delicious-looking dessert for lunch tomorrow? We had to drink that champagne and eat that lovely whatever-it-was before we left, remember.'

'OK, drink the rest of that wine, and I'll refill it from this cold bottle.' Ahmed withdrew the wine from an ice-bucket and held it out.

Twirling the long crystal stem between her fingers, Leonie upended the glass and drank. She said, 'I don't drink a lot of wine, but I could come to like this,' and she held out her glass.

'Yes, I expect you could, but you must remember that this is a special occasion and has to be treated as such,' remarked Ahmed pleasantly, and while she knew what he was referring to, no telltale colour came to stain Leonie's cheeks. She supposed this was the oddest wedding celebration this country of Egypt had ever known.

The man across from her leaned forward to pour the ice-cold liquid, and so close together a glance of glinting emerald-green, and dark sombre blue, met and held for a fraction of eternity. Then Ahmed was quickly, abruptly turning away, and there came to Leonie a jolting thrust as if far away, deep inside her, a lock had been turned. It was buried too deep to even register, and she unconcernedly raised her glass of champagne and drank.

As she did, her gaze swung across the scene about her. She thought wryly that if the gods were looking down and saw this tableau outlined in brilliance against the darkness of the night, they would see what seemingly dreams were made of. A handsome man pouring wine for a girl dressed in a Paris creation, eating dinner in the glamorous surroundings of an exotic country.

If they only knew! she thought, and, setting her empty glass on the table, she said carefully, 'I think I'll turn in, Ahmed. To coin a cliché, it's been a long day.'

CHAPTER THIRTEEN

WHENEVER Leonie remembered those four days sailing back to the Oasis, two memories were superimposed: the leisurely passage up the river in the daytime with their stops at temples and villages—and the presence of Ahmed.

He made the whole journey a time of surface magic; to be with him as they toured the vast temple of Karnak; to listen as he told her—laughing at her interest—about the falcon-headed god Horus; to walk with him through a small Arab village while Suleiman collected fresh supplies, brought only laughter and happiness.

And even on the first day or so, with nothing to do but lie under the canopy, watching the life of the river going on about them, he was always there. And then on the fourth afternoon, with the soft case in which her new possessions had been packed lying beside her, she watched while a sailor brought the launch to a stop. Then they were once again in a dinghy puttering across the water to where their reception committee waited. But this time, Leonie thought more than a little acidly, she was arriving with a band of gold circling one finger.

Greetings were being flung towards them—loud, boisterous to Ahmed's two attendants, then more carefully to Ahmed himself. No one looked at her until Ahmed said, 'This is my wife, the Lady Leonie.'

There were murmured words and nodded heads—both in Arabic and English. She sent her own smile, warm and vibrant, among them all, saying, 'These are different camels.'

They all laughed, and her husband said, 'Yes, they are. The others have been transshipped to their new owners. These are our working animals. Thank goodness you're used to riding, because these beasts aren't as comfortable to ride as the others were.'

Leonie found that in this respect he was right. They were not as comfortable or as smooth a ride as the exquisite racing camels had been. But. . .she grinned to herself as she shifted her body to comply more easily with the gait of the animal beneath her, thinking she had ridden wilder horses which had been more uncomfortable.

'What is that sort of smile in aid of, Leonie?' The words came across to her.

She looked over at her companion riding so easily beside her, and answered, 'I was only thinking I'd had rougher rides.'

He was gazing at her, and this time it was his turn to smile, Leonie who asked sharply, 'Why that smile?'

'*I* was only thinking that you've certainly made up on this ride for the deficiencies of the outer one. This time you won't get sunburnt.'

'No, I won't, will I?' she answered complacently. 'Somebody will find, when they get an account, that all the most expensive cosmetics were bought—including this apricot cream now on my face.'

A loud chuckle of amusement answered her, and white teeth flashed in a dark, tanned face, then Ahmed said, 'Oh, I expect somebody won't find that account too hard to pay.' He must then have checked or directed his camel, because he had slipped back and Hussein came to ride by her side. A swift backward glance saw her new husband conferring with the older, bearded man who was apparently the leader of the party.

Pushing other considerations aside, Leonie enjoyed the journey back. They weren't travelling into a setting sun and it wasn't so hot now. So for the next two hours she gave herself up to riding across the undulating wastes of desert sands. This too she knew she would remember in the years to come—when this episode in her life was past and she was safely back home in Australia.

The cavalcade stopped for only one halt, where she slipped from her kneeling camel to have a cloak fastened about her. And later on, this time when she saw the welcoming lights of the Oasis, she came upon them warm and pleased to have finished the journey.

Zanaide was waiting when they walked into the big living-area, and the table was set with its crystal and silver. She went through to wash as Ahmed was saying, 'We'll have dinner right away, Leonie, Faisal will no doubt have it waiting.'

So, divested of her cloak by Zanaide, face washed of its plethora of sun-screen, she passed again through the curtain-hung opening. She ate what Faisal provided and spoke with him in English, now that he was recognising her presence.

Drinking the thick Turkish coffee which he preferred after dinner, Ahmed spoke carefully. 'I have to live here, in these tents, Leonie, because for a Sheikh of the Wallifa not to dwell in the same quarters as his wife would cause very great comment. But we will manage very well. I will sleep out here on the couch, and only Faisal who has been my body servant all my life attends to these tents.'

Leonie gazed across at him as he smoked one of his little black cigarillos and slowly drank his coffee. His tone and words sounded as if he was discussing some ordinary business deal, not an iota of inflection showing that could cause her embarrassment, so she decided to meet him on his own ground.

And so it was that the next morning she thought acidly that they could be two people married for twenty years—with the exception of having slept together. Ahmed went placidly about the bedroom collecting clothes from his chest, washing and using the brushes on his dressing-table. That was early in the morning before she was up, then, as he breakfasted outside, she was brought in morning tea by Zanaide.

She listened until no more sound penetrated from the next room, then, rising, she dressed in a skirt and blouse and white slip-ons. Moving through to the big room, she walked over and glanced outside to see what a new day was promising. Leaning against a tree there, Mustafa gave a call, and in minutes Faisal arrived with her breakfast.

She ate while thinking she would have to get used to coping again with the chores of ordinary living, once she returned to Australia. No more being waited upon, or having what was practically a maid of her own. She grinned widely at remembering mornings at home, the frantic rush to shower and dress if she had overslept, only the mandatory cup of tea—with a piece of toast if she was lucky, then the rush for the bus.

She rose leisurely from the table and sauntered outside. Thinking she had not been forbidden to do it, she decided she would go for a walk, but Mustafa stopped her. He said in his halting English, 'Put on boots, lady.'

Not understanding him, she asked, puzzled, 'Boots?'

'Yes. . .the Lord Ahmed said there are. . .' Mustafa

was reaching for an unfamiliar word in English, when Faisal's voice cut in,

'Scorpions are found around the trees sometimes.'

Wondering if they thought she was going to indulge in hysterics, Leonie just smiled. She certainly didn't like scorpions, she wouldn't want one to get on her, but she had been brought up in snake country. She went inside to put on her desert boots. With Mustafa following her, she decided she had a guard as well as a maid and a butler. They passed tents, one long brick building, and hundreds of palms. Leonie smiled at people who smiled back at her. She passed what sounded like a school, with children chanting. It took some time to get to where she was making for.

Mustafa spoke a sentence in Arabic, and there was a drawing aside to leave a cleared space. Leonie said hello to Sheikh Ali, receiving a nod in return before he turned sharply to watch the tussle going on in the middle of a fenced circle where a small dark horse was trying to unseat its rider.

Leonie stood back, watching as the youth was thrown. She shook her head. She knew she could tame that little hellion, and as she thought it, she saw Ahmed on the far side. He would know she was here—nothing escaped him. But he was laughing at the discomfited young rider before moving round to where she stood.

'I should have known you would find your way here,' he told her.

'Yes, you should have! I could ride that little mare,' she added, then continued, 'but I suppose I wouldn't be allowed to.'

'You suppose right!' Ahmed said no more, but his tone said it for him. This time she didn't have Mustafa walking along behind her.

'I didn't realise oases could be as large as this one—I mean, out here with only sand about them and no rivers. Why is it that there's water in some places and not in others?'

'I don't think anyone knows that absolutely yet, although everyone has theories. We owe Giles Hailstrom so much for improving our water supply here. That's why we wanted to protect Mrs Hailstrom from getting caught up in the trouble that was brewing last week.'

Two young toddlers ran across the path, and Ahmed moved aside to avoid them. Glancing up at him, trying to wipe away the memory of an episode which that night in Cairo had set in motion, Leonie was unprepared when the small children turned, colliding against her legs.

She was unprepared also at finding herself caught and held tightly, and as she and Ahmed stood fused together, it was as if a lightning bolt had struck, zigzagging around their two immobile forms.

Blue eyes gazed up into those of vivid emerald green only a bare inch away, and Leonie found she couldn't move; that she was being held by a force clamping them together.

A loud shout, and then a gust of boisterous laughter echoed towards them from where the horses were being worked, and she found herself released so suddenly that she staggered back. Ahmed had turned quickly aside. He said, his voice sounding strange, 'We'll go riding this afternoon when it gets cool. You'll like that, won't you?'

'Yes, of course I will. Look, I'm taking you from your work. I'll find my own way to your tents and see about unpacking my clothes from Aswan, and then I might read one of those books I brought back.' Leonie was speaking quickly, her own voice strained and a little breathless.

'You are not taking me away from my work. I will see you back.'

'I really don't need a bodyguard,' she replied rather grimly. 'There's always someone around me.'

'Yes, there is. And until you know your way around that will be the case. You *will* meet my people, and do things; but not all at once.' Ahmed stood aside as she walked through the open tent-flap, but didn't enter behind her.

In the event, she didn't have to unpack the suitcase from Aswan. It had already been done, with clothes hung away and placed into chests. However, both pairs of jeans, the old and the new, had been taken away to be washed.

They did go riding that afternoon, and Leonie found she was riding with a pleasant stranger. A stranger who rode with her and talked about the Oasis and the Arab way of life that went on there. She was aware also, and couldn't do anything about it, that she was replying in the same fashion. The next morning Ahmed wasn't walking back and forth through her bedroom. He was gone!

Faisal, asked as the day wore on, told her that there had been some trouble out in the far desert. . .oh, nothing serious, he had added quickly, observing the look which this news had brought to her face.

She asked for Zanaide to be brought to her, and on her arrival enquired if there was a hospital or school here in which she might be able to work. She couldn't just sit idle all day waiting for the cool of the evening to go riding in. She thought she hated Ahmed.

'Oh yes, lady, there is a school. The Lord Yusef says that anyone who wants to learn may do so—

always, of course, with their father's permission. Aziza teaches in it, and also teaches some English. The Lord Yusef says,' here Zanaide looked carefully at Leonie, 'that the world is changing, and that with the big dam now at Aswan holding all that water, some day it might be able to be piped way out here. . .that is what the Lord Yusef, the Lord Ahmed's father, says.'

I wouldn't mind meeting this Lord Yusef, thought Leonie, then laughed at such thoughts, and said, 'But is there some sort of a hospital, Zanaide? Perhaps I would be able to help there.'

'Oh, no lady! I don't think the Lord Ahmed would like that!'

'Blow the Lord Ahmed,' Leonie said, then, seeing the shocked look on the other girl's face, she smiled. 'I didn't mean that, Zanaide,' she told the girl, 'but I must have something to occupy me. I wonder what the Lord Ahmed would say if I went down to see if I could help with the horses.'

'Oh, no!' This time deep consternation coloured the normally gentle tone of Zanaide's voice. Then she said after a moment's silence, 'Wait, lady,' and went through to the big room. Leonie heard her speaking with Faisal.

'Come with me, lady,' she said happily when she returned. So Leonie judged that she had got permission to take her to wherever they were headed for. And this was where children—of the feminine gender—were seated on carpets spread under shading palms.

'This is the Lady Leonie, Aziza,' said Zanaide, introducing Leonie to the woman facing the class. 'The lady wonders if she could help with some teaching of English. She has time until the Lord Ahmed returns.'

'I will be pleased,' Aziza, who was quite a few years

older than both girls facing her, answered. She was adding, 'The boys sit under the *mullah* at this time of day, so I am trying to teach our girls just the fun. . .fun. . .'

'The fundamentals,' put in Leonie, smiling warmly at the older woman.

'Yes, that is it. Some of these children are orphans, and later they can go on to the Hailstrom School at Aswan.'

And that was where Leonie spent part of her mornings. She found she could make the little girls get their tongues round English words quite well. She also found she was learning some Arabic herself.

And so the days passed, rising leisurely, being waited on, teaching in the mornings, and finding her way about the Oasis. She sometimes looked across at the busy scene where the horses were, but she never went near them. She did go riding on them, however, every afternoon when Ali came to fetch her with two other men in attendance.

And then towards the end of the second week, when Faisal had informed her at breakfast that the Lord Ahmed's task seemed to be finished and that he might be home today, tomorrow, or the next day, Leonie had just turned away, muttering to herself, 'He can go jump!'

He had sent no messages, he had not phoned her, which she now knew he could have done with the radio phone that was housed in the large brick building.

And then the next day a devasating thing happened, sending repercussions among all the men in the Oasis. Ali was late coming to collect her for the afternoon ride. So, ready, she sauntered out to wait. Her young guard, the son of the bearded sheikh who had led their party across the desert to and from the launch, smiled at her. Then, with Ali still not arriving, Leonie decided to walk down to meet him. Their horses, already saddled, were waiting beneath a clump of palms with a youth holding the reins, but the horse circle was empty except for that unbroken little mare she had seen once before—and fallen in love with.

She gazed swiftly around her. No one was about, except for the youth holding their horses, and the young Arab beside that sweating animal in the breaking-in ring. Her guard was speaking with two men far behind. So, swiftly climbing the fence, Leonie walked slowly, oh, so slowly, over to the pair standing quietly in the middle of the dusty ring.

Patting the wet shivering shoulder, Leonie took hold of the reins, ignoring the 'No. . .no, lady!' of the young man holding them. With one foot in the stirrup, she gave a quick jump and was settled in the saddle in seconds flat. She leant over and patted the quivering muscles of the shoulder beneath her, speaking soothingly to the ears standing erect on that small head.

There came a loud shout of alarm. Her guard had seen and was running. It was the worst thing he could have done, and everything happened in a blurring second of time. The loud shout had startled the mare; Ali and others erupted from a nearby tent, and the horse beneath her had jumped, and rearing up sharply, was standing only on its front legs. Leonie laughed, and leant back as far as she could, hitting it lightly on the shoulder with the flat end of her small whip.

The animal came down with a thud, then went up again, this time on his hind hooves. Leaning forward, Leonie laughed out loud, then stopped to give all her attention to thwarting the beast beneath her as it buck-jumped round and round, corkscrewed up and down, trying to dislodge that uninvited burr on its back.

In one of the seconds she had free, Leonie saw the crowd gathered around, Ali and her two attendants inside the open gate of the fenced circle. So suddenly she gave two really hard slaps on the bunched muscles behind her, dug her knees in hard, and shouted.

There was a scatter of bodies as men jumped aside, then they were through the gate, dispersing a fire burning in front of a tent, and with her grip iron-hard to turn the head before her, they had cleared the dwelling and were galloping out in the open desert.

Leonie laughed out loud, bending over to pat the wet shoulder beneath her. She knew she would have to make an effort to turn her mount soon. If she got too far out in the desert she might not find her way back.

She need not have worried. Ali and a circle of others were riding round her on one side, and as she looked, he pointed. Knowing what he meant, she pulled the reins, gently at first, then more firmly, and little by little the mare was turning. And in the distance, further than she would have thought, was the Oasis, silhouetted in the evening sun. With the men behind and around her now, she still let her mount have its tearing way; she wasn't going to give up this exhilarating ride until she had to.

After one look she kept her gaze turned from Ali's scowling face, and she was smiling happily on returning to ride through a press of silent men who made way for her. She rode into the fenced circle and leant over, patting and speaking soothingly to a horse that was now quiet, that had now no intention of buck-jumping at all. Raising her head as the silence all about her continued, she felt her heart jolt.

Ahmed was standing only paces away!

They gazed at one another across the intervening

space and then he was walking towards her. He said through clenched teeth, 'Get down off that horse and go to our tents at once.'

She looked down at him without obeying. How dared he speak to her like that—and in front of everybody too!

Coming yet closer, he said in that soft voice which she had come to know always presaged trouble and which was so low that only she could hear him, 'If you don't come down at once and do as I tell you, I will bring you down and put this whip across your shoulders until you're kneeling in the dirt. . . I promise you!'

She slid down and walked past him, past all the men, who made hurried way for her, and went towards Ahmed's quarters. The bearded father of the youth who had not prevented her from riding the horse followed.

In the big room, too angry to stay still, Leonie paced about. How dared he speak to her as he had done? What terrible wrong had she committed? It was no good telling herself that she knew she could ride the damned animal. She knew in her heart she had been forbidden to do so, and even she, who had made her way alone in a big city, knew also that she was frightened when she remembered the utter ruthlessness in Ahmed's face.

She stopped her pacing as he entered, unhooking the tent-flap so that it dropped into place behind him. Then, facing her, he snapped, 'What in the bloody hell do you think you were doing? Even you, who has to have her own way in everything, should know better than to do what you did!'

The lids which had been half covering his eyes flew

open. And, unable to prevent herself, Leonie fell back a pace. She was gazing into hot, molten anger.

But, angry herself, she flung at him, 'What do you think I was doing? You would know! You would be told! I was only riding a horse. What was so wrong about that?'

'You were riding a horse which had just flung its previous rider against a fence, breaking an arm and three ribs. That was the reason there was no one there to prevent you doing what you did—they were with him. But it wasn't a reason I was prepared to accept. . .'

'It wasn't their fault. It was mine,' interrupted Leonie. 'I wanted to ride it. And what's all this in aid of anyway? I knew I could ride it or I wouldn't have tried. I wouldn't have made myself a laughing stock before your men.' Her eyes were as blazingly angry as were Ahmed's now as she continued, 'I've ridden much wilder horses. . .ones that have been crazier buck-jumpers than that one out there.' She flung out a hand towards the outside.

'You may have in Australia; but this is Egypt, and our women here behave differently. What would have happened if that crazy horse had struck the baby boy who was beside that campfire? What would I have said to his parents?'

Abruptly, the violent lightning of jagged electricity that had been playing about their two angry forms had gone, and a coldness as if coming from a frozen landscape had arrived to take its place.

'There was no one there,' stammered Leonie. 'I would have seen. I could easily have turned the horse.'

'There *was* someone there. . .a baby. And you might have been able to control your mount and you might not! Because at that time, all it was thinking of was getting rid of you. You really do need a lesson you know, Leonie—about the way a proper woman behaves.'

Ahmed was walking towards her—no, stalking in that predatory way he sometimes used, thought Leonie, anger a force emanating from him. She stepped back. But he had reached her, and with one arm clasped behind her back, the other holding the arm she had raised to strike at him, she was brought close into his embrace.

She was being kissed, and not gently either, anger the predominant force behind it all. Then suddenly, as once before had happened, all anger, all violence had departed, and Ahmed's lips on hers were gently moving back and forth. Then he had released her, holding her loosely in his arms before him. His green eyes, gazing at her, were shining, but they held laughter too.

So she said, smiling at him too, 'You smell of camel, Ahmed.'

The laughter in his eyes became ordinary laughter now, echoing from him, and he said, 'I probably do have the aroma of camel about me. I have been riding two whole days to get home—and when I did, look what I found!'

'I'm sorry, Ahmed. I really didn't think that doing such an ordinary thing would cause all this furore.' Then, glancing at his face, still strained, and with the glowing tan showing almost sallow, she said again without thinking, 'You look tired.'

'I am tired! If I hadn't been I wouldn't have spoken to Ali as I did. I can't withdraw the words, so he will probably have to leave here. . .and he was my second father.'

'Oh, no, Ahmed!'

Leonie received no reply. She said then, her own face strained now, 'Would it make any difference if I went and apologised? Said that it was my fault?'

Leaning indolently against a tall cupboard now, Ahmed was looking her over. 'I imagine if you went like that it would certainly cause some sort of a reaction—whether it would be the one you were aiming for is another matter.' That tired voice was carrying almost a hint of amusement now.

'You haven't said no, and if you want to be childish you can be—however, I'll just tidy myself.' Leonie brushed down her jeans, saw that her blouse was straight and covering them, combed the hair she had just brushed. She thought better not even lipstick, and turned for the open tent-flap, which Ahmed had fastened back.

Faisal was there with Zanaide, waiting for her, and they walked, the three of them, through a section of the Oasis she had not seen before. They came to a stop before a large double tent. Ali came out to meet them, and Leonie said, 'I'm sorry for what I did, Sheikh Ali. It was foolish of me. Could I be forgiven?'

For a moment, the fierce bearded face just looked at her, then, as Leonie's nervous system gave a relieved sigh, Sheikh Ali had given a small nod and raised a hand palm outwards.

Leonie nodded herself and turned, then swung back, saying, 'I'm sorry I caused trouble. . .but I'm not sorry I rode the horse. That ride out in the desert was something I won't forget.' There didn't seem to be any need for translating these words, because she was answered at once in Arabic, then Zanaide told her, 'The Sheikh Ali says, lady, that you rode well.'

Leonie walked back to her husband's tents, happier than she had been for some time. From that fierce old man, those words had been a compliment.

CHAPTER FOURTEEN

When she re-entered the bedroom, Ahmed was coming through the heavy bathroom curtain, a white djibbah covering him. He stopped before the dressing-table to brush still wet hair, then drew out a burnous from a standing cupboard. It was not created in the voluminous white which Leonie remembered, but in the black and silver of the Wallifa colours.

She stood just inside the opening as he settled the enveloping garment about him and finished adding the usual men's accoutrements to an inside pocket. He hadn't spoken one word before, but now he turned, saying, 'I didn't ask because your look said everything for you! What did Ali say?'

'He nodded and raised his hand. . .and,' continued Leonie defiantly, 'he told me I rode well!'

'Did he, now! Well, you can take that as a compliment. But I tell you, and I mean it, Leonie, it was a stupid thing to do.'

He didn't wait for her to answer his stricture, he was adding, 'Now, for my sins, I have to go and give an account of my mission. I have news for them. . .' He broke off after looking at her more carefully to say sharply, 'You look pale. . .are you all right?'

'Of course I'm all right, and I am not pale!' Leonie almost spat at him, knowing, without wanting the man opposite to know, that suddenly her legs were shaking. It was only the delayed reaction of the fight with the horse, and that violent emotional scene after it. She moved to lean indolently against one of the big cupboards, as her companion had done earlier. 'Of course I'm OK,' she repeated.

'I have to go. I don't want to be too late, because all I'd like to do is fall into bed for a week,' here, unexpectedly that wicked pirate's glint came to colour his eyes as he added, 'preferably in there.' An outflung arm showed her where. Then that hand was turned in farewell, and the room was abruptly empty of his presence.

'Oh, well,' she muttered, pushing herself away from her leaning post, and like Ahmed, when she returned from her wash she also donned a loose comfortable garment. But this caftan was in the vivid blues and greens that coloured the ocean of Surfers Paradise at home. She also thought, examining her reflection in the mirror, that this creation was going to be another expensive item on an account somebody was going to have to pay.

Faisal was hovering when she went out. She smiled at him, saying, 'Aren't you going to this affair, Faisal?'

'Yes, lady. . .after.'

'You can go now. Everything I want is there. I only drink coffee because of the Lord Ahmed, so you haven't to bother with that. Go!'

He gave one last glance around and departed. Leonie heard him speak, and a voice which sounded like Hussein's answering.

She finished eating all she wanted, cleared and stacked dishes as she would have at home, leaving them on the trolley. She switched off the main light, leaving the one burning at the far end, and went inside. Undressed, she settled down with pillows banked behind her to read.

She didn't know what had aroused her. She woke abruptly from a sleep she had unexpectedly fallen into.

Her bedlamp was still burning. Then she heard it again: a great shout rising up. Slipping out of bed, she went cautiously through to the open tent-flap and glanced outside.

Nothing or no one was in evidence except Hussein, and he was turned away, gazing down through the Oasis. No apprehension marred his stance, so the shouting she could hear more clearly now had apparently brought no alarm.

Then out of the night, almost frightening in its intensive violence, came a thunder of rapidly moving hooves, and amid a great shower of scattering sand a fiery chestnut horse was pulled from a lunging gallop to an abrupt halt. It ended upright on its hind legs.

Not wishful to be seen, Leonie kept herself hidden. She couldn't see the rider as he slid down from a mount now standing with heaving chest. The tone of that rider's voice didn't sound at all like Ahmed's, but certainly no one else would be there.

Gliding like a silent shadow through to the bedroom as the figure came towards the open tent-flap, Leonie watched as it lifted a hand to unhook and drop the heavy material. . .and staggered. She came out of hiding.

She gazed at a face which looked different, then noticed that the normally immaculate hair was dishevelled, more than one lock hanging down over his forehead. She also saw that his eyes were brilliant gleaming emerald pinpoints, and that a hand went out to hold on to the tent side. She remembered the slurred voice that had greeted Hussein, and knew now why it had not sounded like his own.

She said, without realising she had said it, 'You're drunk!'

Across the small space separating them, he gazed at

her. He said, 'Do you know, I think you may be right! But if Ali didn't know I can ride any horse that was ever foaled, drunk or sober, he certainly knows now.'

'Oh. . . Was that one of the unbroken ones?' was all Leonie could find to say.

'It was! But that little episode was just a small revenge I could cope with.' Here, Ahmed moved unsteadily and almost fell into a chair. 'But the other little bit of revenge was a different matter. We are forbidden alcohol, but nothing was said by Mohammed about a mixture made from palm-hearts and dates, and which is, my dear Leonie, more potent than any alcohol I've ever drunk. I really think half the Oasis is drunk tonight.'

The slurred words stopped, and raising his head, Ahmed said, 'I think a bath is indicated.' Leonie grinned, delighted that for once Ahmed wasn't in control of every little thing.

Glittering green eyes met laughing blue ones, then Ahmed rose. Leonie laughed, and standing back, watched the upright figure that was moving as if trying to walk a painted line. And then, sitting cross-legged on the bed, she heard the sound of splashing for a long time. When he reappeared he wore a large bath-towel wrapped sarong-fashion about him.

Looking fully at her, he said curtly, 'Enjoy yourself for this once, Leonie, for you will never come in contact with its like again. For your information, I don't drink, except for the occasional social drink, or champagne sometimes. Tonight's little affair was a case of saving face—Ali's face. He knows I hate the stuff. However, I expect he just decided to pay me back for that earlier trouble.'

'Good heavens, what childish games!' interrupted Leonie, amazed. 'Couldn't you just apologise and say that anger and tiredness caused you to speak to him as you did. . .'

Her words stopped abruptly. She had seen those black eyebrows rise practically to his hairline before Ahmed interrupted in his turn, 'Don't be silly, Leonie. There's no way I could ever take back words once spoken. . . And Ali wouldn't expect me to. A paramount sheikh of the Wallifa *never* considers himself in the wrong!'

Leonie could find nothing with which to answer these words as her companion stepped past her, but she followed as he walked his straight line back to the couch. He lay down, his face buried in the cushions, his eyes shut.

She stood, undecided, then went to one of the carved chests and collected a blanket, throwing it over him. Ahmed neither moved nor spoke. Leonie went to her own bed and slept.

When next she surfaced to the real world about her, Ahmed was sitting on the side of the bed. Her glance roving his features that showed none of the laughter of last night, she told him, 'You don't look as healthy as I've seen you look, but you seem better this morning.'

'I am! And a wash and tea will complete the cure. However. . .' Ahmed paused for a moment, then said, 'Leonie, I have just received word that some members of the Government accompanied by Army engineers are arriving today. I normally give them lunch or dinner. I think that this time, however, it will have to be the latter. I being who I am, they will know I'm married, so do you think. . .could you. . .?' This hesitation was so unlike Ahmed that she said sharply,

'What is it you want of me, Ahmed? To preside at your table, or hide myself away?'

Ahmed grinned. 'I don't think they would expect

me to hide you away. I really haven't got a harem. No, I was wondering if you'd put on your prettiest dress and make them all jealous of me.'

It was Leonie's turn to smile this time. 'I can just imagine anyone being jealous of you because of me! They probably all have beautiful wives, or *they* might have harems. . .'

Ahmed laughed, and unexpectedly he was the old familiar Ahmed. She asked softly, 'What dress shall I wear?' and it was her now laughing as she said, 'Do you think they'd like a certain blue one I possess? Someone I once knew remarked upon it!'

'And about you looking like an ice maiden in it. I remember! But I think not for this dinner. I do think, however, they could be very jealous of me if you were to entertain them looking as you do now.'

And abruptly between them there was that familiar threaded cord of silken steel holding them together. Leonie felt the warm rush of rose-pink that came to stain both cheeks and neck. . . Ahmed rose and left the room.

Leonie remained seated, arms hugging drawn-up knees, fair shining hair cascading from a downbent head. What was going to come of this situation? she wondered. Ahmed *could* have asked her to marry him before all this happened—but he hadn't!

There had to be some reason. He liked her. . .wanted her, but. . . Unable to guess where these thoughts were leading her, unable to decide on anything, Leonie slipped from the bed. The noise she had heard from the other room had gone now. Probably Ahmed was drinking his tea. She glanced down at the thin cotton nightdress held up with only shoestring straps. She had no dressing-gown, only a short towelling beach-coat that doubled for one. It wouldn't do to go out there, where Faisal might come in.

Deliberately, she walked over to one of Ahmed's clothes chests and took out a white djibbah. Slipping it over her head, she didn't bother with any black and silver cord this time, then, with a comb through her hair, she made her way into the living-room.

Black eyebrows raised sky-high received her. She told him astringently, 'I don't have anything else, and as I thought you would want the other room, I've borrowed this to come out here.'

'I've used the room with you in it before. That didn't hassle me.'

'I also thought I'd like a cup of tea.'

Ahmed gazed from the large breakfast cup he held, and a glinting smile coloured his eyes a deeper emerald. 'There's none left,' he told her, 'but Faisal will be back in a second. Order your breakfast.' A hand half raised, he left, taking his teacup with him.

'Oh, I hate him!' she muttered, then wondered how many times she had said those same words. However, Faisal did come, and she did order her breakfast. She drank the cold orange juice, and some tea, and was sitting back in her chair swinging a bare foot back and forth when her husband came through the curtained opening. He came dressed as a working man, in khaki slacks and shirt, and he was rolling the long sleeves above the elbows.

'I'm coming,' he called back in English to a shout in Arabic from outside. 'The helicopter is here,' he told her. 'We should be home fairly early. They won't want to stay late.' He looked at her, over all of her. . .and smiled. He raised a hand, said, 'Don't forget—look beautiful,' and was gone.

Levering herself upright, Leonie returned to the bedroom, rehung Ahmed's djibbah, then leisurely shampooed her hair, towelled it as dry as she could and combed it in place. She spent the rest of the morning teaching, and most of the afternoon watching large bunches of dates being harvested.

Then with reluctance, knowing it was time to begin dressing, she walked slowly back to their own quarters. . .and stared in amazement. At the front of the big tents a vividly coloured carpet had been spread, and set upon it was a carved table laid with gleaming crystal and silver. Also, not one tent-flap but two were folded back and tied to a roof stanchion, allowing the inside space to form a backdrop. The whole scene gave an overall impression of Oriental splendour.

While dressing she heard the cavalcade go through to the centre of the Oasis, and half an hour or so later was just brushing on blue eye-shadow when Ahmed entered like a cyclone, unbuttoning and unfastening as he came. He went through to wash, and in minutes was back, taking no notice of her as he changed into a cream linen suit.

Proceeding with her own toilette, finishing the outline of her lips with a deep pink lipstick, Leonie gazed into the mirror and moved restlessly. Ahmed was standing close behind her. But before she could protest, his hands were lifting.

She felt something cool settle about her throat, and tanned fingers were arranging a double string of pearls that fell to below her breasts, setting straight the blue clasp that fastened them. He pulled her back to lean against him, saying, 'These should have been given to you after that ceremony in Cairo—except I thought you might have thrown them at me if I had done so. Also this. . .'

He reached down to bring up her left hand and slid a ring on to it, to lie against the engraved gold band. 'That clasp is turquoise to match this,' he was telling her, and Leonie found herself looking at a stone of deep blue set within a circle of dull gold. It was not a modern ring; it looked years old. . .antique.

Ahmed was saying now, his lips resting against her hair, 'Do you know, Leonie, that the ancient Egyptians and their women wore turquoise in many ornaments? They looked on it as almost a magic stone—and even today, women tie a blue bead of it on their babies to keep away the evil eye. Do you think these two stones will keep away any evil that might come near you?'

'Ahmed, I can't!' Leonie wasn't laughing with him.

'If you are going to say you can't accept them, don't be silly, Leonie. Even our poorest families have jewellery of some sort.'

She knew that, but these gleaming ropes of pearls! She gazed helplessly up at him.

'Would you also object if I said you look beautiful?'

She gazed at the face of a Greek god above her, and her lips twisted wryly. She knew who looked beautiful.

Ahmed swung her round, saying, 'Well, here we go. . .to entertain our first guests.' So they went to stand just inside the tent entrance: the girl in her ivory crêpe wedding dress, and the tall dark handsome man in cream linen.

Their guests came, and Leonie had her hand taken and bowed over, and said how do you do in return. But she did smile warmly at Ibrahaim Pasha, whom she remembered from another occasion.

The dinner was served in both Occidental and Oriental cuisine. And in spite of some nervousness, Leonie found she was enjoying herself. But she kept her glance away from the amusement in her husband's gaze as he took in the all too evident admiration in one of the younger Egyptians' face and manner.

They ate their dinner and the moon came up. In one of the small lulls in the conversation, Leonie glanced out and saw it, not full, but shedding its radiance of silver and ebony. Unexpectedly, she was out in that same desert watching another moonlit sky. She moved sharply, almost knocking over her water glass. But mostly she sat silent listening to the conversation going on around her. The talk, of course, was of water, the substance more precious than gold up here. The coffee arrived, and they didn't move into the lounge area, but only drew a little back from the table to drink the thick Turkish brew. The young officer and Ibrahaim Pasha drank brandy in big balloon glasses with theirs, the other two nothing. They, like Ahmed, had not drunk any of the wine provided either.

Leonie wondered if this was policy—or if he was still feeling the results of the night before.

Then suddenly the senior member of the party made a move, and Leonie found herself standing beside her husband as farewells were said, the large desert-type carriage taking them on their way. Ahmed neither spoke nor touched her until the vehicle with its escort of Wallifa warriors had departed.

He took her hand then and, parting the curtain that shielded the bedroom, drew her through. Taking both her hands, he held them wide, saying, 'Did you enjoy entertaining your first party of guests?' And on receiving no reply he went on, the laughter disappearing from his eyes, 'I've told you at other times how much I want you. Can I tell you now that you are the essence of my life. . .and by Allah, I can't go on any longer with this farce we're living!'

He brought her to him, and Leonie felt the tremor that ran through the tense hard body, but she pulled back, stammering, 'You never told me that. . .you always drew back from any declaration. What was I to think?'

'My father was in Europe, and my uncle in Khartoum on tribal business. My situation is difficult, Leonie, and I wanted to inform them first. I am important to the Wallifa, and both of them would have preferred me to marry among my own, and to tell you the truth I think I would probably have done so if one day I hadn't looked across a crowded airport. . .'

The arm around her tightened still more until their two bodies were standing together, length against length, with hollows and curves fusing them into one entity; with the thudding of the man's heart, like galloping hooves of the desert, sending its message through to every nerve-end.

Then unexpectedly he set her back, two arms clasped loosely behind her holding her prisoner. He said, and there was now even a hint of laughter in his words, 'Wasn't there some kind of a promise you exacted, and a further promise from me that I would abide by it, except for. . .'

Leonie felt the tide of burning colour that rushed to stain her skin, and muttered to herself, 'If he thinks I'm going to brazenly ask him to make love to me, he'd better think again!'

'Well. . .?' asked that inexorable voice.

Still, if she wouldn't ask him, she could show him. She sent herself back into his body, closer than she had been before, melting her entire length into his, then, on high-heeled sandals, reached up to clasp her hands behind his neck. She found herself being kissed. . .not hard, not demandingly, but in slow, heartbreaking caresses that were dragging her very soul from her.

It was Ahmed who brought to an end those timeless,

drugged caresses, and with a voice strained and slurred said, 'I think I'd better go and have a cigarillo, because if I keep on the way I'm behaving now, we will have a repetition of that explosive episode we went through on the first night you came to the Oasis. And I can't allow that!'

But Leonie pressed into him even more tightly, saying, 'I don't care, Ahmed.'

'Do you not?' he enquired with a raised eyebrow. 'Very well, then, here we go. . . But first. . .' He reached behind her and ran down a zip, and the French creation that was her wedding dress lay in a pool around her feet. The rest of her clothes followed, and his voice, still in that slurred tone, said, 'And that is how it should be: the shining lustre of pearls your only covering.'

She was swung up and laid on the pillows, where she found herself abandoned. But for only a moment. A match was struck, a flare of orange light came to be the only illumination, giving brightness to the silent space around them. Then Ahmed was beside her. He didn't begin with kisses, he lay with an arm just holding her prisoner to him. He didn't speak either, he only made love to her. All the times she had been with him—on the launch that first morning, on the small balcony at Shepheards, in the moonlit desert, and of course here. . .coalesced into this magic moment.

Once she caught hold of his hand and held it, saying, 'No. . .' and knew Ahmed had answered her, but she only shook her head, knowing that those roving caresses which made her every nerve and pulse jump and soar were carrying her into a new dimension.

Then, when his lips took over, she arched completely into what was now all she remembered of existence, and from somewhere far away she heard him say, 'Bear with me if I do not perform as gently as I might, but the waiting has been too long.'

And abruptly Leonie was giving herself to a whirl-pool that gathered her up and up, sending her reaching for heights she felt she must grasp. . . Then later, drifting, she found herself in Ahmed's arms, hearing the hurried, frantic breathing that told its own story.

She waited, and the silent room around her waited too. Then as the man beside her didn't speak, she did. 'Will I make any difference to your life, Ahmed? Will my presence affect the way you have to live?'

And once again he was laughing. He said, 'Stop it, Leonie. I haven't the breath left to laugh. Will you make any difference to my life, indeed! Without you in it, all it would be to me would be dust and ashes.'

Astounded, frightened even at such words, Leonie said haltingly, 'I didn't mean about that, although. . .although, Ahmed, I always thought it was only I who had such feelings. No. . . I meant among the Wallifa.'

'I don't think so, because in my fashion I am very needed. But I do wish that damned Hassan would get himself married. And do you know, essence of my heart. . .' Astounded, delighted at this Arabic endear-ment, Leonie noted thankfully that that frightening tone had gone, amusement taking its place as Ahmed continued, 'I think the Sheikh Ahmed, my uncle, will only have to see you riding one of our unbroken horses, and he will make you a member of the Wallifa, with or without my consent. Does that answer your question?

'But that, my beloved, will most certainly have to wait. So for now. . .' Amusement gone, the deep timbre of passion and want taking over the tone of a voice whose every nuance she had come to know sent her arching towards him.

And as the slow minutes were counted away second by second, desire came to colour the dim, quiet tent about them. Once Leonie spoke. . . Once Ahmed answered, then was silent, and only a flickering orange flame was there to etch their moving figures against darkness. Such a small light to watch over them as they travelled their own pathway to journey's end.

Harlequin Superromance®

Available in Superromance this month
#462—STARLIT PROMISE

STARLIT PROMISE is a deeply moving story of a
woman coming to terms with her grief and gradually
opening her heart to life and love.

Author Petra Holland sets the scene beautifully, never
allowing her heroine to become mired in self-pity. It
is a story that will touch your heart and leave you
celebrating the strength of the human spirit.

Available wherever Harlequin books
are sold.

Harlequin Intrigue®

Trust No One...

When you are outwitting a cunning killer, confronting dark secrets or unmasking a devious imposter, it's hard to know whom to trust. Strong arms reach out to embrace you—but are they a safe harbor...or a tiger's den?

When you're on the run, do you dare to fall in love?

For heart-stopping suspense and heart-stirring romance, read Harlequin Intrigue. Two new titles each month.

HARLEQUIN INTRIGUE—where you can expect the unexpected.

Harlequin Superromance®

CHILDREN OF THE HEART
by Sally Garrett

Available this month

Romance readers the world over have wept and
rejoiced over Sally Garrett's heartwarming stories of
love, caring and commitment. In her new novel,
Children of the Heart, Sally once again weaves a story
that will touch your most tender emotions.

You'll be moved to tears of joy

Nearly two hundred children have passed through
Trenance McKay's foster home. But after her husband
leaves her, Trenance knows she'll always have to
struggle alone. No man could have enough room in his
heart both for Trenance and for so many needy
children. Max Tulley, news anchor for KSPO TV is
willing to try, but how long can his love last?

"Sally Garrett does some of the best character studies
in the genre and will not disappoint her fans."
Romantic Times

**Look for *Children of the Heart* wherever
Harlequin Romance novels are sold.** SCH

HARLEQUIN

Romance®

This September, travel to England
with Harlequin Romance
FIRST CLASS title #3149,
ROSES HAVE THORNS
by Betty Neels

FIRST CLASS

It was Radolf Nauta's fault that Sarah lost her job at the hospital and was forced to look elsewhere for a living. So she wasn't
particulary pleased to meet him again in a totally different environment. Not that he seemed disposed to be gracious to her:
arrogant, opinionated and entirely too sure of himself, Radolf
was just the sort of man Sarah disliked most. And yet, the
more she saw of him, the more she found herself wondering
what he really thought about her—which was stupid, because
he was the last man on earth she could ever love....